Sara's

Surprise

Thousand Islands Brides

Book 2

by

Susan G Mathis

smWordWorks

Fiction

Published by smWordworks

www.SusanGMathis.com

Editor: Denise Weimer

Cover design: Julia Evans

This book is a work of fiction. Names, characters, places, incidents, and dialogues are either products of the author's imagination or used fictitiously. Any resemblance to actual persons, living or dead, events or locales is coincidental.

Scripture quotations from The Authorized (King James) Version. Rights in the Authorized Version in the United Kingdom are vested in the Crown. Reproduced by permission of the Crown's patentee, Cambridge University Press.

Printed in the United States of America

To sign up for Susan's newsletter

and find out about upcoming books

and other fun stuff,

visit www.SusanGMathis.com.

PRAISE FOR SARA'S SURPRISE

An authentic and engaging look at the lives of servants during the Gilded Age, Sara's Surprise takes us to the picturesque Thousand Islands. Author Susan Mathis delicately weaves in the historic setting as well as the challenges faced when dreams could be threatened by the more powerful. A delightful and heartwarming tale of romance and redemption, Sara's Surprise is a Christmas story whose captivating characters will keep you enthralled. ~Marilyn Turk, author of historical novels

Sara's Surprise is the delightful tale of a young woman reaching for her dream. A romantic setting and compelling characters, including a precocious little girl, make this an enchanting story you'll love. ~Vickie McDonough, author of 50 books, including *The Anonymous Bride*.

Sara's Surprise is a Christmas tale of perseverance, hope, and love—perfect for a quick holiday read. ~Davalynn Spencer, author of The Front Range Brides books

A poignant story filled with lessons and love. Set in the picturesque beauty of the Thousand Islands of upstate New York, this heartwarming story will draw you into the world of the rich and famous of the Gilded Age." ~Tiffany Amber Stockton, author of over 25 novels, including A Fair to Remember (September 2019)

Sara's Surprise is a charming tale of new beginnings set in 1873. Sara, the new assistant pastry chef, and Sean, the front desk manager at the elegant Crossmon House Hotel will face some unexpected challenges before reaching their sweet ending. This engaging story has timeless elements that will bring many smiles.~Janet Grunst, author of *A Heart Set Free* and *A Heart For Freedom*.

Sara's Surprise is a sweet romance that will capture readers with its lovable characters. Tenacious and kind, Sara O'Neill desires to become an independent and a successful pastry chef. Feisty little Madison Graham, who needs a mother, charms Sara. And Madison's dad, Sean Graham, is the kind of man who is worthy of her regard. Their story will warm your heart this winter. Highly recommended! ~Kathleen Rouser, author of *Rumors and Promises*

A charming story sure to delight, *Sara's Surprise* takes readers through a journey of delectable French pastries and the challenges of trust and destiny. Reminiscent of favorite Hallmark romances! ~Brandy Vallance, award-winning author of *The Covered Deep* & *Within the Veil*

Sara's Surprise kept me turning pages in this heartwarming tale of lives changed by our Jeremiah 29:11's God. ~Donna Schlachter, author of *Double Jeopardy* and other historicals

Sara's Surprise is an engaging romp into the past, with winsome characters and a sweet love story that captures the heart. ~Sherrinda Ketchersid, author of *Lord of Her Heart*

Susan Mathis is a talented writer who intertwines a lovely story with details of exquisite French pastry baking and even gives recipes at the end. I couldn't put the book down! ~Donna Gawell, author of historical fiction including *In the Shadow of Salem*

DEDICATION

To my wonderful daughter, Janelle, who inspires me with her zest for life and has blessed me with four precious granddaughters, Reagan, Madison, Devyn, and Peyton. Each one of you is a gift from heaven. And to Madison whose spunky, inquisitive, lovable personality inspired the character of the same name.

ACKNOWLEDGMENTS

I hope you enjoy *Sara's Surprise*. If you've read any of my other books, you know that I love introducing history to my readers through fictional stories. I hope this story sparks interest in our amazing past, especially the fascinating past of the marvelous Thousand Islands.

In researching the Crossmon House Hotel, I heard from several folks whose family members worked in the hotel. I even received some pretty cool photos, one of a room key of that era. Thanks to you, my readers, for your faithful support and for staying connected.

Thanks to Judy Keeler, my wonderful historical editor who combs through my manuscripts for accuracy. Because of her, you can trust that my stories are historically correct.

Thanks to my fabulous editor, Denise Weimer, for being the mentor I've always dreamed of and for sharing your talents with me.

To my amazing beta readers, Laurie, Davalynn, and Barb, for all your hard work and wise input, thank you. And to all my dear friends who have journeyed with me in my writing, thank you.

To my husband, Dale, who inspires my heroes because you are my hero.

Thanks for your emails, social media posts, and especially for your reviews. Most of all, thanks for your friendship. Please stay in touch at <u>susan@susangmathis.com</u>.

CHAPTER 1

Alexandria Bay, New York

July 1873

The St. Lawrence River sparkled in the early morning sunshine as Sara O'Neill walked toward her new life at the elegant Crossmon House Hotel. An abundant variety of colorful flowers and blooming bushes decorated the entrance. She took in a magical whiff of nature's loveliest fragrances as she climbed the grand staircase leading to the lobby. On her first day of employment, she wanted to walk through the front doors and experience the grandeur of the famous hotel like an upper-class guest. Just this once.

"Please, miss. Allow me." A wee girl popped into her path. Where did she come from? Sara glanced at the nearby bush and grinned. The child pulled open the heavy, leaded-glass door with all her might, grunting and nearly losing her balance. Sara tossed her a smile and a nod as she passed over the threshold. The little girl grinned back, a full four—or was it more?—teeth missing.

That explained her adorable lisp.

Sara let out an amused giggle. "Thank you, sweet girl." They stepped into the grand lobby dotted with tall pillars, small tables, velvet sofas, and a large front desk. To the left of the desk, a wide staircase led to the upper floors, and to the right was a hallway leading to the elegant dining room where, even from where she stood, Sara could see diners would enjoy a beautiful river view. She scanned the huge room but saw no one nearby. "Where's your mama?"

The child shook her honey-brown curls, a huge bow wobbling precariously on top of her head. "Haven't got one."

"Your nanny?" A chill ran down Sara's spine. Such a beautiful little girl should not be alone in public.

"Haven't one of those neither." The girl blinked and shrugged. She crossed her arms as her gaze slid to the marble floor.

Sara patted her small shoulders, her white eyelet dress soft to the touch. "Well, now, what are you doing here?" She peeked around a large pillar to scan the lobby again, but at the moment, only one man stood behind the front desk, his back to them.

"I work here. Leastwise, when school's out. What's your name, miss?" The child grinned, her blue eyes twinkling.

Her precociousness surprised Sara, warmed her cheeks, and drew a smile to her lips. What a delightful wee one! "I'm Sara O'Neill, and I work here too. In the kitchen."

Curls bouncing with another shake of her head, the girl pursed her lips, rolling her eyes. "Chef has a temper as hot as his stove, but Mister LaFleur is oh, so handsome. I'm going to marry him when I get big." With this confession, she clasped her hands to her heart as if she might swoon.

Sara held back a grin, but she couldn't hide her amusement. "I see. So what's your name, little beauty?" A bit of honey might go a long way with this imp.

"Madison Graham, and I'm seven." She thrust her hands on her hips and tilted her head as if to challenge Sara.

She wouldn't disappoint. "Well, you're a very grownup seven, to be sure." Sara put out her hand to shake Madison's tiny one, but instead, the child dove into her arms and gave her a tight and most overwhelming hug.

"I'm happy to have a new friend working here, Miss O'Neill." Madison held tight as she looked up at Sara, her small face angelic.

Sara gave her a gentle squeeze before touching her cheek and releasing her. She stepped back and nodded. "Me, too, but I mustn't be late for work." She bent down and straightened the child's crooked hair bow. "So nice to meet you."

Madison grabbed her hand and pulled her from behind the pillar toward the kitchen. "No, you mustn't be late. Chef'd have your head on a platter."

"Where have you been, darlin'? I've been looking all over for you." The man who'd been behind the desk was now in front of them. His handsome face sported a well-trimmed mustache and beard the color of brandy. He turned to her and bowed, gazing at her with eyes the same color as his hair but with a hundred flecks of gold. "Sean Graham, Crossmon House front desk manager. And this little lady's papa. And who are you?"

~ ~ ~

Sean tweaked Madison's chin as his gaze darted to and fro looking for a husband belonging to the woman before him. Her simple gray garb and dark-blonde hair pulled into a low, twisted chignon spoke of the working class, far outside the status of Crossmon guests. Her thin, pink lips turned up into a gentle smile. Who was this petite beauty paying such tender heed to his daughter?

She daintily curtsied. "Sara O'Neill, sir. I'm pleased to meet you and to work as day staff in the Crossmon kitchen. Your Miss Madison gave me a warm welcome on my first day." Sara's soft-gray eyes twinkled as she winked at his daughter, who rewarded her with the cute toothless grin he loved so much.

His heart thumped faster as he tried to mask his alarm. Staff always entered through the back, not through the grand entrance. He kept his tone casual. "Ah … welcome to Crossmon, miss. Or is it missus?"

The woman blinked as her face took on a pretty, pink hue the same color as Madison's dress. "Miss."

"Aye. Good to meet you, Miss O'Neill. I hope you'll enjoy your time with us. The Crossmons are a fine couple to work for, and this large, new addition to the hotel offers the most modern conveniences. We cater to families and expect that many of our nearly three hundred patrons will return year after year."

Sara nodded. "That's wonderful."

Sean glanced to the desk to make sure no one needed his attention just then. "I suppose that, since Cook is a man of few words, he wasn't keen to give you a tour? And he obviously forgot tell you that staff only use the back entrance."

Sara's eyes grew wide as she shook her head, her face flushing a bright red. "No. I'm sorry. I've only seen the kitchen when I interviewed last week. And here." She glanced around the lobby. "I'll be sure to use only the kitchen entrance from now on." She fidgeted, shifting from foot to foot.

He waved off his scolding. "'Tis fine. This time." He winked, hoping to calm her. Instead, a visible shiver ran through her from head to toe. Sean tried again. "I'll be happy to show you around if no one else does. You'll be on the day shift like me, aye?"

"Yes. Here at six sharp. I mustn't be late." Her eyes darted toward the kitchen.

Sean checked the massive grandfather clock just feet from where they stood, his eyes growing wide. He waved an arm toward the kitchen and took hold of his daughter's hand with the other lest she attempt to follow Miss O'Neill. "We mustn't keep you, then. Chef requires perfect punctuality."

Sara gave another quick curtsy and said, "Yes, well, nice to meet you both" before scurrying toward the kitchen.

Madison pulled his hand and looked up at him. "Papa, why was she so nervous? And why is your face so red?"

~ ~ ~

Sara closed the kitchen door behind her as smells of fresh baked bread, bacon, sausage, coffee, and fried eggs filled her senses. Then her breath caught when she

17

laid eyes on the tray of the prettiest baked goods she'd ever seen. Oh to be able to create such works of art one day. She scanned the room full of impeccable, modern kitchen equipment. And just a year ago, she'd thought the Pullmans' kitchen was well-equipped.

"Miss O'Neill, I assume?" She snapped her head toward a swarthy man with a deep voice. Not Chef's. The chef who'd interviewed her was short and stocky and not at all handsome.

"Yes, sir?" Sara curtsied.

"I am Jacque LaFleur, pastry chef for this fine establishment. I have requested that you be my assistant pastry chef, as I'm told you've had a measure of experience and such a position will fulfill a lifelong dream of yours. Besides, the previous assistant left just yesterday to care for her aging parents."

Sara sucked in a deep breath and held it. Could this be happening? So soon?

When she'd interviewed with the master chef, she'd told him that one day she would like to learn the trade. But never in her wildest dreams did she think she'd be given the position of assistant pastry chef here and now. On her first day?

Sara let out her breath and curtsied again, trying to recover from the shock. "Yes, sir. I mean, I've dreamed of learning the art ever since I worked on Pullman Island last summer."

She scanned the handsome face before her. The man's jet-black hair and mustache contrasted with his clean-shaven skin and pale blue eyes. His piercing stare caused her heart to beat wildly, and she swallowed hard.

LaFleur took hold of her hands and placed a slow kiss on the palms of both of them. Then he repeated the kisses again. Rather than her heart calming, it sped up like a bird taking flight. She carefully slipped her hands from his grasp and pulled them behind her back, interlacing them tight for an extra measure of protection.

LaFleur waved as if conducting an orchestra. "I shall teach you the ways of a *patissier*. A pastry chef!" With that announcement, he bowed low, one hand behind his back and one over his stomach. His gregariousness set Sara's teeth on edge. "I was trained at the finest culinary arts school in Montreal, *Academie Culinaire*, and, I might add, was awarded the highest honors of this most beloved of all station chefs. I have experience in creating the finest of Quebec's eclectic *mélange* of French pastries, and I now bring the wonders of preparing breads and pastries, *croissant* and *petit fours*, fondue and chocolate *éclairs* to you."

Sara blinked. "Thank you, sir."

He clicked his heels together and stood like a wooden soldier, not breaking his seriousness for a moment. "Call me Chef LaFleur. Let us begin!"

Sara nodded, dipping her chin. What a high-minded, handsome Frenchman she'd be working for. "*Oui*, Chef LaFleur." Maybe a bit of French would settle him down. Last summer, her co-worker, Claudia, had taught her a dozen words. Sara had enjoyed learning them, locking them tight in her memory.

LaFleur's dark brows raised, and his thin lips almost turned upward—but not quite. He waved her over to an impeccable marble-topped table, and Sara gingerly stepped forward, waiting for his command. This man would be not only her employer but also instructor, and she trembled to think she'd be found wanting from the start. What did she know about French baking?

During Sara's spare moments in the Pullman Island kitchen, Claudia had shown her a thing or two, but she was never formally trained. And she certainly hadn't the skills of Chef LaFleur. Besides, this French-Canadian was the most handsome man she'd ever laid her eyes on. How would she manage?

Chef LaFleur puffed out his chest, giving it a thump. "Mr. Crossmon chose me from a lengthy list of candidates, and I shall bring fame and fortune to the proprietor and his property. We will create culinary masterpieces of epic gastronomy, but it will take an assistant who will listen and learn, will do as I command, and will not stray from my instruction. Will you be that person, Miss O'Neill?"

Sara squared her shoulders and nodded. "Oui, Chef LaFleur. Under the lessons of Mr. Pullman's cook, I came to know the ways of the kitchen, though not such a grand one as this. But I shall try to meet your standards, sir."

Chef LaFleur patted her shoulder and then slid his hand down her back and gave it a quick stroke, sending shivers through her. Though she had heard the

French were affectionate, the man's touch nearly sent her to her knees. Besides, he was her superior.

He pulled her from her thoughts. "In the afternoon, you shall also help with the high tea, bringing food and drink to the servers."

Sara nodded. "I'd be honored, sir."

For most of the morning, Sara met the rest of the kitchen staff and followed Chef LaFleur around the pastry station, growing accustomed to the kitchen and plans for making marvelous French pastries and bread. A dozen or more times throughout the lesson, he casually, almost absentmindedly, touched her arm, her hair, her back.

Each time, Sara grew more reticent. When he came too close, she discreetly stepped back, but more often than not, he moved closer as if she were a magnet attracting a piece of iron. By lunchtime, her breath whooshed out with a deep exhale when he set her to knead a large bowl of bread dough while, at the other end of the table, he decorated tiny petit fours for the afternoon tea.

As she kneaded her nervousness into the dough, Chef LaFleur waxed eloquent about making the perfect rosebud petit fours. "I choose to use a simple butter cake, splitting the layer and adding this wonderful raspberry filling." He scooped a finger full of the mixture, came near and leaned across the table, and then thrust it toward her mouth. "Taste!" It wasn't a suggestion.

Sara reluctantly opened her mouth. Chef LaFleur slipped his finger between her teeth, commanding she fully taste it. She closed her lips and withdrew, swallowing the truly delightful fruity mixture past the lump in her throat. "It's lovely."

"*Non*. It is spectacular!" He waved his hand and went to the sink to wash it.

What was she to do with such a man? He'd invaded her space all morning and now invaded *her*! She held back tears as the morning's fears and frustrations built within and threatened to overpower her. "If you'll excuse me, Chef LaFleur. I must visit the ladies' room."

He nodded, drying his hands on a towel and returning to their workstation. "It is time for lunch, *mademoiselle*. Cover the dough, and take your break. Then return to ready for the tea."

Sara kneaded the last bit of dough, laid it in the bowl, and covered it. After washing her hands, she glanced at Chef LaFleur, relieved he worked on the far end of the table, adding the tiny rosebud decorations to the tops of the petit fours that were already covered with perfect, pale yellow, green, and pink frosting. Indeed, they were a marvel!

Sara filled her tin cup with water and stopped by the restroom before stepping outside to find the sun high in the sky and humidity hovering thick in the air. She found a quiet grassy spot under a large oak tree and sat down with her lunch pail.

As she munched on carrots and a simple jam sandwich, she mulled the morning's events over in her head. Surely, Chef LaFleur meant no harm. It was just his Frenchness. But how would she endure such invasion of her privacy?

CHAPTER 2

Though Sara's brow moistened with the heat of the day, she shuddered. "Help me, Lord. Please keep me safe, and let me learn from this talented man. You have a plan; let Your will be done this summer."

"Are you praying, Miss O'Neill? I pray too." Madison stepped under the tree and plunked down beside her. She promptly picked a dandelion and thrust it in Sara's face. "For your first day."

Sara took the weed and waved it under the child's chin. "Ahhh, I see you like butter."

Madison scrunched up her face. Her wide eyes and furrowed brow told Sara she wasn't familiar with the old wives' tale. "How do you know?"

"If you hold a dandelion or buttercup under your chin and it reflects the yellow, you like butter. But if it doesn't, you don't. Would you like to share a butter and jam sandwich with me?"

Madison's nodded furiously. "Oh, that would be delightful. Papa made me eat carrots and a piece of chicken." Her nose scrunched up, and then she huffed. "Men."

Sara's tension broke free into a bubbling giggle. "Aye, men. And what have you been doing this fine morning?"

Madison took a quarter of the sandwich Sara handed her, taking a tiny bite and swallowing before she spoke. "I got to be in the burro brigade. It was my second time, 'cuz only three other children showed up." She scooted to sit on her haunches, her hands on her lap. Her eyes fairly danced. But that toothless smile? Irresistible.

"What's the burro brigade, wee one? I'm not familiar with it."

The child shifted and plunked back down on her bottom. "Mr. Crossmon loves kids, so he bought a bunch of donkeys and a trained goat for us children to ride. I only get to ride if not enough kids come, like today. But I get to show the new kids how to ride on their backs or in the carts if they're scaredy-cats. Mr. and Mrs. Crossmon are very nice and let me work with

Papa in the summertime 'cuz the Crossmon House is a family hotel. The missus calls me the 'ambassador to the wee ones.'"

"Really? That's quite an honor, Miss Madison."

The little girl swatted at a mosquito. "Yes, it is. But when I'm behind the desk with Papa, he says I must be quiet as a mouse, and that's hard to do. I'm not a mouse, you see."

"I see that." Sara waved away a swarm of mosquitoes hovering around the child's head. "You must be sweet as honey. They don't want to leave you be."

"They bite too. Look!" Madison rolled up her sleeve and turned her arm over to reveal several red spots. "Five." She displayed her five fingers. "And they itch."

Sara patted her arm and pulled the sleeve back down. "I know. But they will heal."

"So how is Chef LaFleur? Isn't he wonderful?" Madison covered her heart with her small hand and rolled her eyes to the sky. "What's he making for tea today? If the patrons don't eat them all, I get to taste one of the pastries."

"Do you, now? He's making petit fours, tiny cakes that have a *surprise* in the middle." Sara made the surprise sound as valuable as gold.

Just then, the door opened, and Madison's father appeared. "There you are." He smiled at his daughter and turned to Sara. "Is she bothering you?"

"No, sir. She's keeping me company, and it feels as though I've spent my luncheon with a little princess." She snapped a smile at the child, who flashed her toothless grin back.

~ ~ ~

Sean stepped under the shade of the tree and wiped his brow. "I'm pleased you feel that way. She's a darling, but she can be ... a wee bit of a nuisance. She's been known to get herself into mischief in two shakes of a lamb's tail."

"Papa!" Madison squealed out a protest.

He grinned, shrugging his shoulders. "So how was your first morning in the Crossmon kitchens?"

Sara scrambled to find an appropriate answer, looking out at the river. Was she buying some time? "I've been given the position of assistant pastry chef."

Sean's right cheek began to twitch and knew his eyes grew stormy. He balled his hands into a fist and then unclenched them. Twice. "I hadn't heard that." He glanced at Madison and back at Sara. "Congratulations." His tone was flat. Ominous. As it should be. Why would LaFleur choose Sara to assist him? He knew why.

Madison tilted her little head. Was she confused at her father's sudden change in mood? Sara should be.

Sara began fidgeting, her lips turned down as if she might cry. Did LaFleur already give her reason to worry? The rogue had best treat Sara well, or he'd …

Sara sighed and drew back her skirts to stand, but Sean held out his hand to help her. She took it, and her frown turned into a beaming smile. He tossed a similar smile her way.

"I'll help too." Madison took Sara's other arm and hoisted her up as if she were an invalid, nearly pulling her off balance.

"Careful, darling. Don't hurt Miss O'Neill."

Sara chuckled. "She's fine. Thank you both." She wiped a few stray hairs from her forehead and smoothed her skirts. "I'd better get back to the kitchen. I am to help with the afternoon tea service."

Wonderful! Sean bowed low and then bid her to walk ahead of him. "I will see you later, then. Afternoon teas are served in the parlor adjoining the lobby." As he stole another glance at Sara, he suddenly realized that he hadn't been so attracted to a woman since his dear Matilda left this earth.

Madison clapped her hands. "Then I'll see you too. Papa makes me rest in the tiny office behind the desk when days are hot." She shot him an annoyed pout, one she'd tried to use on him many times. It wouldn't work.

"You have far too much freedom already, my wee lassie. Be grateful you have as much as you do." Sean gave her a hug before he opened the door and let Sara and his daughter pass through it before he did. He gave Sara an eye roll that he knew smacked of adoration for the imp.

Sara raised an eyebrow, nodding agreement. "She's delightful, sir. You must have your hands full day and night."

"How right you are, Miss O'Neill." His neck grew hot, and he adjusted his collar. What did she think of him as a father, letting his daughter run free day after day?

~ ~ ~

Sara bobbed a curtsy, wished Sean and Madison a good day, and scurried to the kitchen, her heart racing.

Before long, Sara was tasked to place a variety of tiny sandwiches on several three-tiered crystal and silver trays. Flower-shaped cucumber sandwiches. Triangular chicken salad ones. And square cream cheese and smoked salmon sandwiches. Perfect. She covered each tier with clean napkins and turned to the dessert trays.

The same three-tiered trays awaited sweets— chocolate-covered nuts, pastries, mints, molded chocolates—and the petit fours. But how should she place them? She did the best she could, but as she put them on the tray, Chef LaFleur came from behind and slapped her hand. Hard. He knocked a chocolate out of her grasp, causing it to roll on the floor. "Non! Not like that!" He huffed and shot a disapproving look, his eyes full of fire. "Look what you did!" He stomped over to

31

the chocolate, picking it up and throwing it in the trash with angry force. "Do you know nothing?"

"I … I'm sorry, sir. I will learn." Sara's eyes smarted with tears. Would she lose her job the first day she got it? "I … I want to learn, Chef LaFleur, but I've never done a formal afternoon tea service before."

Her words seemed to take the fire from the man as fast as it was lit. He blew out a breath and lifted his head. "Very well, then. I shall instruct you." He patted her back as he would a child's, giving her a condescending scowl.

Sara swallowed. "Th-thank you."

"Sweets and nuts do not co-exist on the same plate, mademoiselle. Non! And my magnificent creations must outshine them all. Two of the same color must not adjoin one another. This is a work of art, mademoiselle, and that art must overwhelm the guests with its beauty. The palate must be overcome with lust for every bite!"

Lust? Dear me. The seriousness of Chef LaFleur's speech sounded silly to Sara's ears. She held back a giggle, biting the inside of her cheek to keep from laughing and trying to keep her eyes from revealing her amusement. "I see, Chef LaFleur. Thank you for the wise counsel, *monsieur*."

He smiled, tilting his chin in reception of her compliment. Then he reached out and touched her cheek with the back of his hand, sweeping it downward and pausing at her jawline. "I see you know how to learn. That is good, *mon cheri*."

Sara squeaked of protest. His darling? Never! She stepped back and wiped her hands on her apron. "I think I can manage this now."

"Oui. Carry on, then. I shall return before tea service begins."

She scrambled over to the sink to wash her hands, anything to remove the veil of disgust that enveloped her just then. Chef LaFleur whisked out the door, relief pouring over Sara like a gentle breeze.

Returning to the table, Sara finished the trays, happy to work in peace, even though her normally steady hand betrayed her. She adjusted a pink petit four on the last tray, covered it with a cloth, and wondered what to do next.

Breathe. Pray. Rest.

She did just that as the kitchen staff hummed around her like a swarm of buzzing bees. They acknowledged her, even smiled, but no one talked to her. She was the newest staff member, and although everyone—even Cook—seemed pleasant enough, their eyes betrayed them. Was it sadness, concern, even caution she saw? Whatever it was, her churning belly told her it wasn't good.

Before long, Chef LaFleur returned through the main door leading to the lobby and parlor. "It is time to serve the afternoon tea, mademoiselle!" He sidled up to Sara, running his hand down the full length of her arm and giving her a scrutinizing frown, setting every nerve on edge. "You must change into your serving dress. Although you shall not serve, the patrons must not see you in this." He grabbed a piece of her sleeve, catching a bit of her skin with it. With a smirk and narrowed eyes, he pinched a bit harder.

Sara yelped and took a big step back, bumping hard into a table. What was that for? She rubbed the small of her back, willing the pain away. Then she rubbed her arm, holding back her frustration. "I wasn't given another uniform, monsieur."

34

Chef LaFleur let out a deep huff, went to a closet on the far side of the kitchen, and retrieved a deep-blue dress and a stiffly starched, frilly white apron with a matching mobcap. "This should fit you. Bring it with you every day, clean and pressed. Impeccable! You must never be unpresentable, mademoiselle."

"Oui, Chef LaFleur. I'll change and be right back." Before her superior could say more, Sara hurried to the staff ladies' room. Tears spilled onto her cheeks as she changed her clothes, but she hadn't time to think. She brushed them away and rushed back to the kitchen.

When she returned, the room was a flurry of activity. Kitchen maids scurried around, arranging delicate vases of fresh-cut flowers and creamers and sugar bowls on silver trays. Fine china teapots steamed on several other silver trays of the same intricate design as the tiered trays she'd filled with the tea sweets.

Chef LaFleur stood with a scowl on his face and hand on his hips. "Too long. Our patrons await their service. Off with you, and deliver the tea first. Then the savory tiers. Then the delights. Go!"

"Go where, sir? Where should I take them? Surely, not to the tables." Sara's heart beat faster. She wouldn't have to serve the hotel patrons after all, would she?

"Foolish girl. To the service table in the lobby. The waiters wait the tables. Do you know nothing?" He pushed her toward the tea trays.

Sara carefully picked up one of the heavy trays with three teapots on it, trying not to spill as her hands shook.

How could he expect her to know things when he didn't tell her? How dare he? She gnashed her teeth, attempting to disseminate her frustration.

Once in the lobby, Sara could see where she was to set the tea—a long, finely decorated table adorned with flowers and a lacy tablecloth. Two waiters in perfect livery stood like soldiers at attention. She set the tray on the table and removed the pots, careful not to spill any tea on the lace. As she started to return to the kitchen, something latched around her ankles.

Sara squeaked out a high-pitched "ah!" before clamping her mouth closed. Snapping her gaze downward, she discovered Madison looking up with a mischievous grin, still holding tight to her while the tablecloth draped over the back half of the girl's body.

"Good afternoon, Miss O'Neill. Papa thinks I'm sleeping in the office, but I couldn't sleep. I wanted to say hello to you." The imp gazed into the parlor, where about a dozen fancily dressed women waited for tea. She released Sara's legs and grinned again. "I think I might get some treats. But it's so hard to wait." Her pretty little pout drew a smile from Sara.

"I must be about my work, wee one. I'll try to save you something special. Now go back to your papa, else he mightn't let you have any. And remember to be quiet as a mouse." Sara glanced toward the front desk and picked up her empty tray to return to the kitchen.

"I will." Madison scooted out from under the table and tiptoed toward the office unnoticed by her father.

Sara nodded her off with a whisper. "See you later, Madison Mouse."

Madison giggled, putting her finger to her lips, and disappeared into the office.

Their pleasant moment together proved short-lived. Chef LaFleur met Sara at the kitchen door, his face red and eyes blazing. "What are you doing, playing with that child when you should be working?"

CHAPTER 3

After leaving the safety of Ann's Café, Sara walked along the boardwalk to her second day at the Crossmon House. She was grateful to spend the summer in the peacefulness of the widow's spare room instead of the staff quarters, especially since Chef LaFleur resided there. But where would she go when the summer season ended? Sara sighed. She'd ponder that another day.

Still smarting from yesterday's scolding from the livid Chef LaFleur, Sara prayed this would be a new day, a good day. During the five-minute walk through the center of town, she enjoyed the early morning mist along the St. Lawrence River. She passed several businesses, still closed and quiet. A rooster crowed in the distance, and the smell of wild roses, honeysuckle, and lilacs wafted in the breeze. Perhaps it'd be a better day, after all.

Upon opening the rear kitchen door, she nearly bumped into an elegant woman who was likely in her fifties, her silvery hair swept into a simple style. The scent of lemony perfume swirled around her. Why would such a fine lady be entering the kitchen so early in the morning?

Sara's face burned at her clumsiness. "Oh. Excuse me, madam."

The woman's pleasant smile promptly put her at ease. "Good morning, miss. I haven't had the pleasure of meeting you. I'm Mrs. Crossmon."

Sara curtsied low, but when she rose, she realized the missus had her hand out. Should she shake it or kiss it? She shook it. "Pleased to make your acquaintance, ma'am. I'm Sara O'Neill, assistant to the pastry chef."

"Are you now? And such a pretty young thing." Mrs. Crossmon tilted her head, putting a finger to her temple. "Say, does your father have a farm out on Old Goose Bay?"

Sara blinked. "He did. He and Mother passed last winter." How did Mrs. Crossmon know him?

"Oh, I am sorry for your loss." Mrs. Crossmon's eyes grew tender, compassionate. "I went to primary school with him ages ago. I grew up here in the bay, you know. Such a studious lad he was, and always a gentleman. Haven't seen him in years."

"Thank you, ma'am." Sara shot a glance at the pastry station. The missus must've noticed, for she took one of Sara's hands and gave it a gentle squeeze.

"Dear me, I do prattle on so. I mustn't keep you from your work even if I do own the place." She let out the sweetest giggle Sara had ever heard from an older woman before opening the door to exit. "Have a good day, dear."

Sara curtsied. "You have a lovely day, too, missus. It was a pleasure to make your acquaintance." She closed the kitchen door with a smile lingering on her face but was accosted by her boss the moment she turned.

"You are speaking to Mrs. Crossmon? Who do you think you are, *fille*?" Chef LaFleur grabbed her arm, squeezing it hard, likely bruising her, pulling her to the pastry table.

Sara sucked in a breath. "I'm sorry, sir. She addressed me first."

Chef's narrowed eyes reminded her of a feral cat ready to pounce on a mouse. And she was the mouse.

He shook his head. "She is the proprietor's wife." He huffed. "And you are … nothing." He huffed again. "Do not cross her path again, mademoiselle, or you shall hear from me." Chef LaFleur took a wooden spoon and gave the table one harsh rap. "Let us begin. Today we shall make Éclairs au Chocolate and Lemon Madelines."

As if he hadn't just scolded her, bruised her, threatened her, Chef LaFleur took on his calm, almost charming, instructor persona that she'd seen yesterday. As if he were two different men. He picked up a large saltshaker and held it up. "What is this, mademoiselle?"

"Salt?"

"Non! It is the spice of life. It is one of the oldest spices in the entire world, a basic necessity for enhancing food to make it fit for human taste buds. It is ... *magnifique*!" He waved the shaker in the air.

Sara bit her lip, almost longing for the days of working under the Pullmans' cook. She might have been harsh at times, but she was never cruel or so unpredictable.

Chef LaFleur narrowed his eyes at her, thrusting the saltshaker toward her. "To be a cook, you must learn to use this well. You must taste your creations before you bake them. Your palate must *comprend*."

He opened a fancy wooden box and pulled out a dark chocolate bonbon with an intricate swirl of white on it. "Taste." He pushed it toward her and would have rammed it in her face if Sara hadn't promptly parted her lips. He stuffed the entire bonbon into her mouth. "Taste! Savor." He plunked his hands on his hips and waited while she self-consciously chewed the rich confectionary, nearly choking on it as she swallowed.

"Well?"

"Monsieur?"

"What do you think of it?"

"It's wonderful, Chef LaFleur." Sara's words rang hollow in her ears. Though it was a delectable treat, him shoving the entire thing into her mouth and impatiently waiting for her to assess it yielded a bitter aftertaste.

"Non, you ignorant imbecile! What is missing? What?" He took up the wooden spoon and gave the table another bang, silencing the entire kitchen. Sara glanced at Cook and saw that all of the kitchen staff stared at her. "Look at me, mademoiselle. I am your teacher!"

Sara snapped her eyes back to him, her face burning as if a hot oven had scorched it. She frantically searched for understanding. What was missing? How should she know? Her eyes smarted, and her bottom lip began to quiver. She grasped for the only thing they'd been talking about. "Salt?"

"Oui! *Fabuleux*! You may not be as witless as I thought. My former assistant left out the salt in these bonbons. A tragic mistake. Unforgivable. They were ruined for anyone of status. The cultured palate *comprend*."

Suddenly, he stopped his tirade and thrust a notecard in her face. "We will start with a most simple recipe. Lemon Madelines." She took it from his hands. "Gather the ingredients. Now."

"Oui, monsieur." Sara hurried to find the butter, eggs, sugar, and other ingredients. Bringing them back to the table, she set them in order of the recipe.

Chef LaFleur took up an egg. "Where did you get this?"

"From the ice box." Where else would she get it?

"Non! Did you learn nothing under the Pullman employ? You must know that butter and eggs must not be cold. Room temperature makes the batter fluffy and light. Cold eggs will seize the batter into chunks of goo. Non! Get them from over there." He pointed an accusing finger toward the stove, eyeing the eggs. "Take these away!"

With a quivering sigh, Sara scurried to the stove, where Cook stirred a savory soup in a large pot. Sara nodded toward the eggs. "May I take four, please?"

The short, stocky man nodded and patted her forearm gently. "Of course." His eyes darted toward Chef LaFleur. "This is not about you. He is a genius at what he does but creates quite a stir in the process."

Sara nearly cried at his empathy. "Thank you." She took the eggs and returned to the pastry station, Chef nowhere to be found. Pleased to have the freedom to do her work, she created the Madeleine recipe without receiving more of Chef's ire and put the batter in the icebox.

Once it had chilled, she poured the batter into the molds, baked them, and after they cooled, she dusted them with confectioners' sugar.

Chef returned and reached around her from behind, picked up a still warm cookie, and gave a whiff. "Magnifique, mademoiselle!" He surveyed it and popped the entire thing in his mouth, smacking his lips noisily.

"*Délicieux*. Well done. Now we must create Éclairs au Chocolate, a much more complicated recipe." He handed Sara the directions, broken into three parts—the *pâte à choux*, pastry cream, and chocolate glaze.

Chef interrupted her reading. "Let us begin with the *pâte à choux* —the éclair dough. You must observe this time, for the next, you shall do it yourself."

"Oui, monsieur." Sara watched as he boiled a mixture until it no longer stuck to the spoon. He put the dough into a bowl and added eggs one at a time as Sara stirred, but as soon as she stopped, he fairly growled a scolding. "Continue! The dough must be glossy and smooth."

Sara shuddered, taking a tiny step away from him in case he tried to manhandle her again. Her heart raced, and the lump in her throat threatened to choke her. She swallowed back her fears.

Once the mixture was done, Chef bid her to fill a pastry bag and pipe out sixteen five-inch tubes of dough. The first few were rather lopsided, but once she got the hang of it, the rest were almost perfect. While they baked, Chef created the pastry cream and had her make the chocolate glaze.

"Keep your station clear, mademoiselle!" He swept his hand along the tabletop, spilling flour and sugar in his wake and sending pieces of shaved chocolate flying to the floor. "Clean this up before I return from my meeting."

Was Chef compelled to harass her? Though the Pullman Island cook had been strict, Sara had never feared she'd be harmed. Never thought she was a continual failure. Never had her nerves set on edge the entire day. Not like this. Why was this man so cruel?

Sara hurried to wash the dishes and clean her station. And the mess Chef had made.

By teatime, Chef had berated and yelled at her until the occasional sprinkling of compliments did nothing to sooth the abuse. Placing the best éclairs and Lemon Madelines on a large silver tray, Sara proudly carried them to the tea table, tossing Mr. Graham a smile. How refreshing to see a friendly face at last!

~ ~ ~

Sean had waited all afternoon to catch a glimpse of Sara. Indeed, Madison had fallen asleep waiting as well. He'd looked for the lovely new assistant pastry chef at lunchtime, yet here she was with the prettiest smile he'd seen in a long time. Relieved he had no guests at the front desk, he joined Sara at the tea table. "Good afternoon, Miss O'Neill. I hope your morning was a pleasant one."

Sara nodded as she set the tray on the table, but her eyes betrayed her. Was it fear or sadness he saw in them? "And to you, sir. Where's the little miss?"

"Please call me Sean. Madison fell asleep waiting to see you. She nearly drove me mad." Sean gave her a sheepish grin and shrugged. "I had to confine her to the office and caught her … twice … trying to sneak into the kitchen. What spell did you cast over her, miss?" He wouldn't mention that he'd wracked his brain to think of an excuse to go to the kitchen and see her as well.

Sara giggled. "Call me Sara. No spell, I just 'spect she senses how much I like her, 'tis all." She shot a glance at the kitchen and lifted her tray. "I must get back. Chef gets displeased when I dally."

"When are you finished with work? Might Madison and I have the privilege of walking you home? She will never forgive me if she doesn't see you." Sean held his breath awaiting her reply.

Sara gave a quick curtsy. "I'm through at five, and I'd be honored to see her, sir."

"Very good. See you then."

Honored to see Madison? What about him? Maybe on their stroll he could get to know her a bit and land a place in her heart, as his daughter apparently had. He watched her return to the kitchen, then went back to the desk with a prayer for success on the evening's walk.

~ ~ ~

Sean addressed Sara as they turned onto Alex Bay's Main Street, with its towering trees and lush lawns. "Where to?"

"I'm staying above Ann's Café near the end of town. Ann was a dear friend of my mama's, so I'm letting a room from her." Sadness marred Sara's pretty face.

"Tell me about your family, please." Sean prayed he wasn't opening a tender wound.

Sara told him about her parents dying of pneumonia within days of each other last winter. She talked about her family farm outside of town, now overseen by her grumpy uncle. And she shared about her brother, Thomas, who was married to her best friend, Katelyn. But at last, Sara's eyes twinkled when she revealed that the couple still worked on Pullman Island even though Katelyn was expecting their first child around Christmastime.

Sean swallowed. "You've had quite a troubling year, lass. Sorry about your parents and your farm."

Sara's lips lifted to a half smile. "Thank you. And you? What about you and your wee lassie?"

"We hail from Watertown, where I worked at the Woodruff Hotel until Mr. Crossmon invited me to serve here. My wife passed just days after childbirth, and it was no easy task taking care of this precious bundle of joy alone in the big city." He paused, glancing at his daughter, who seemed lost in her daydreams. "I'd been looking for us to move to a smaller town for some time and have always loved the river, so this was a perfect opportunity for a new start."

"Well, I'm glad you're here." Her voice held a hint of excitement, or was it uncertainty?

Sean bobbed his head. "And I'm glad to hear about your best friend and brother."

"I don't have a brother." Madison interjected the comment as she slipped her right hand into Sara's left and her left hand into his, swinging their arms with delight. "So far, it's just been Papa and me."

"Careful, darlin'. You don't want to hurt Miss O'Neill's arm."

Madison's eyes grew large, and her tiny mouth made an O. "Sorry. I'd never hurt you on purpose. I just get excited, 'tis all. I like being in between you two. Walking with Papa is nice, but having a lady here is even better."

Sara flushed and giggled nervously as she swung Madison's arm. "I like being with you, too, sweet lassie. You really are altogether adorable."

"'Praise the young and they will flourish.' I think this Irish Proverb is true, especially in the case of my little darlin'." Sean winked at Madison.

Sara smiled at him, lifting an eyebrow, her eyes twinkling. She mouthed a suggestion for the two of them to swing Madison.

What a fine idea!

He nodded and counted. "One. Two. Three." Together, they swung the child off her feet and into the air.

Madison's face filled with delight as she squealed. "Wheeeeee.! That was fun. Again. Please?"

As they complied, Sara had the same delightful expression as Madison. They could almost pass as mother and daughter. Sean sucked in a breath, shocked by his thoughts. He had to bring the moment back to reality.

"Enough, darlin'." He stopped the swinging but winked. "Miss O'Neill had a long day's work, and we mustn't tucker her out more." He gave Madison a narrow-eyed warning. She could be persistent when she wanted something. Before she could complain, he turned to Sara. "How was your day in the kitchen?"

Sara swallowed hard, and her brow furrowed. Was she unhappy? She shook her head as if avoiding a swarm of gnats. "I'm … learning a lot." Her voice sounded flat. Unsure. Uneasy.

Was Chef LaFleur tormenting Sara as he had the last assistant? If so, he'd regret the day he stepped into the Crossmon kitchen. Such a sweet, innocent, and vulnerable young woman as Sara needed a protector, someone to look out for her as he looked out for his lassie. But would she even want him to take on such a role?

CHAPTER 4

The new day had barely begun, but trouble was brewing. Sara hurried to stop Madison from entering the kitchen. She bent down to whisper in the child's ear, alarm ringing in her words. "You mustn't be in here, wee one. Chef LaFleur would be displeased." She scooted the child behind her as Chef shut the pantry door and turned their way. "Hurry, child! Run back to the lobby before he sees you."

"But why?" Madison's pursed lips and furrowed brows revealed her innocent confusion. "I work here too."

"Under your father's care, yes, but not here in the kitchen. It's too ... dangerous." Sara shot a glance at Chef coming their way and shooed her out the door. "Now go to your father. I'll see you later."

Sara closed the door behind the girl. Then she sauntered up to the pastry table as if nothing had happened, her heart racing. Chef's tight jaw and dark stare revealed that he saw past her shallow ruse. She grabbed a rag and furiously began cleaning the countertop.

"I have eyes everywhere, mademoiselle, and trying to hide that troublesome *enfant* might be grounds for dismissal. If it happens again, you will leave my employ. Understood?"

"Oui, Chef LaFleur." Sara's voice quivered. She bit the inside of her cheek as she stared at the floor. "I'm sorry, sir."

He grabbed her wrist and pulled her close until she could smell alcohol on his breath. "You must heed my instructions. All of them." He gave her arm a little twist before releasing it.

Sara rubbed her wrist, willing the pain away. But with it came fear that seeped deep into her bones. Was Chef a drunkard? Was that why he changed personalities so fast? Her grandfather had possessed the same dual personality and struggled with "demon liquor," as Mama had called it. Maybe that explained his duplicitous nature.

"Are you listening to me?" Chef slapped the table, pulling Sara from her musings.

"Sir? Oui, monsieur." She held her breath, praying he wouldn't ask her what he'd just said.

Thankfully, he didn't. He gave his apron a tug to straighten it and adjusted his *toque*, the close-fitting chef's hat he always wore. "This morning, we shall make *calissons*, the traditional French candy that came from Aix-en-Provence, where my grandparents were famous for making the delights. Let us begin."

Sara had never made candy before, didn't even know what *calissons* were, but she wouldn't admit that to Chef. What would he do if he knew how incompetent she really was? He set her to chopping and combining candied melon, orange peel, and almonds. Then she added a few drops of orange flower water and honey to the mixture.

"The paste must be smooth and pale yellow. Once it is, roll out the dough to a half-inch thick. We will leave it to dry overnight and finish the creation tomorrow."

Sara did as he bid her and set the tray aside. Then she made a batch of butter cookies while Chef created beautiful dark chocolate truffles rolled in nuts. Her mouth watered at the sight. How she wished she could taste just one ... without it being shoved into her mouth. Instead of asking to try one, she tidied her station to perfection and washed her hands.

Chef finished and came over to survey her *calissons* dough and butter cookies with a scrutinizing stare. "Very good. Take your lunch, and then we will make small ramekins of *crème brûlée* for today's tea. Return in thirty minutes."

Sara tugged off her apron and hurried out the door. She had to speak with Sean whether she tamed her growling stomach or not.

~ ~ ~

Sean tossed Sara a smile as he finished checking in an elderly couple and called for the bellhop. Once they left the desk, he turned his attention to the young lass before him. Her pale complexion alarmed him. Moreover, she nervously tucked hair behind her ear and chewed on her lip. Her eyes held worry. Or was it fear?

"Good day, Sara. Are you unwell? Might it help to partake of your lunch in the quiet of my office?"

Sara nodded. "Thank you, sir. And I must speak to you about an important matter if you can spare a moment."

Sean motioned her toward his office behind the front desk. He pulled out his desk chair and bid her to sit. He gave her shoulder a quick pat before stepping back. Just touching her sent lightning bolts up his arm and into his brain. Just as he had felt with Madison's mother.

He cleared his throat, hoping to clear his mind as well. "Madison may return at any moment, and I'll have guests arriving soon. What is it you need to say, miss?"

Sara looked down at her hands, clenched so tightly her knuckles were white. "You know I adore your daughter, but we have a bit of a problem."

Sean rolled his eyes. The older his daughter got, the more mischief she seemed to find. Blathers! The hotel was no place for a child, especially in the busy summertime, but what could he do? He could not afford a nanny and had no family to care for her. He sighed. "What has she done now?"

"Purely innocent, I'm sure, but she came into the kitchen today to see me, and Chef was displeased."

"Chef is all stuff and nonsense. That man puts on more airs than the king of England. Give it no heed." *Keep it light, ol' boy, and you'll not upset her further.* Yet her eyes told another tale.

"He said I'd lose my position if she came in again." Sara's voice quivered, and he longed to take her in his arms and comfort her.

No! Sara's not a child. Sean squared his shoulders and swallowed hard. "I'll make sure Madison doesn't stick a toenail in the kitchen ever again. You'll not lose your job because of her."

Sara blew out a breath, color returning to her cheeks. "Thank you, kind sir. Please don't let her know I spoke of this."

"Spoke about what?" Madison appeared in the doorjamb, her mischievous grin casting sunshine into the tiny office. "Papa, there's a big man at the counter. Better see to him."

Sean chuckled. His lassie was just too big for her petticoats. "Thank you, darlin'. Why don't you join Miss Sara for lunch?"

Sara smiled and nodded. "Yes. Please do."

~ ~ ~

Sara ate her hard-boiled egg and tomato while she listened to the lassie prattle on about chasing a bullfrog with a boy named Christopher. But before she could hear more about Madison's childish adventures, Sara realized her time was up. "I'm sorry to leave so soon, but I only had a few minutes for lunch today. Have a good afternoon."

"I'll come with you. I have more tales to tell you." Madison wiped the jam off her face and stepped her way.

Sara bent down, shaking her head. "No, Miss Madison. You mustn't enter the kitchen. Did you see Chef LaFleur's face this morning?"

Madison nodded, paused, and then shrugged her shoulders. "All right. But I don't like it one bit."

Sara patted her head and laughed. "Neither do I, sweet girl. Neither do I."

Chef LaFleur was waiting for her when she returned, arms folded over his chest, eyes narrowed. "Did I not say thirty minutes? You are late." He glanced at the clock on the wall. She followed his gaze.

One minute late.

"Gather the ramekins, and let us make the crème brûlée."

Sara hurried to grab the tray of petite, white, fluted ramekins she'd already readied. Bringing them to the pastry station, she set them down, waiting for further instructions.

"I will teach you to separate eggs the proper way. I noticed you drew them from shell to shell. That is incorrect. You pour them onto your palm like this." Chef broke an egg with one hand and let the egg white run through his fingers in one fluid motion. He plopped the yolk in a bowl. "Now you try."

Sara cracked an egg with one hand. But before she adjusted the shell and got her hand under the egg, the white fell to the table in a gooey mess. She panicked, and the yolk broke too.

"Imbecile! Non! You don't even know how to break an egg." He slapped her hand and showed her again, making the process look simple. Effortless.

"I'm sorry, monsieur. I will learn." Sara blinked back tears and tried again, this time accomplishing the feat, albeit rather awkwardly.

Chef took her through the next steps of heating the cream to "temper the eggs and prevent them from scrambling." At his instruction, she gently mixed in the remaining ingredients, simmered it, and poured the custard into the dishes.

Chef LaFleur handed her a tea towel. "You must put a towel in the bottom of the pan and fill it halfway with water before baking."

Sara did as he commanded her, baked them, cooled and chilled them, and grinned with pride at her accomplishment. Just before teatime, Chef pulled her away from preparing the teapots to show her the final step.

He took her hand and led her back to the pastry table, touching her arm as if he was courting her. She shivered even though it must've been ninety degrees in the kitchen.

"For the final presentation, we sprinkle sugar on top of the custard to create a lovely caramelized crust. We put them under the broiler for a few moments and *voilà*! They will be magnifique." He put his fingers together and touched his lips to the tips, fanning out his hand as if to send some magical kiss to the heavens.

Sara wished he'd wash his hands instead.

Thankfully, the crème brûlée was picture perfect, and after he placed a sprig of mint and three blackberries on top of each one, they were a work of art. Chef LaFleur may be persnickety, but he sure was talented.

Once her workday was finished, Sara found Madison under the tree in the back, arms crossed, her bottom lip stuck out in a most dreadful pout.

"What's the matter, wee one? I thought you were having a fine day." Sara squatted down to her level.

Madison snapped her eyes and looked at Sara and then snapped them right back out to the river. "I was ... until Papa found out he had to work late. And I can no longer be free to roam the hotel as I have. Someone"—she looked back at Sara and glared at her—"complained about me. Again. Can't a body have any fun?"

Sara took her hand and patted it. "There. There. I know it's hard, but many children have it much worse." An idea came to her, and she stuck a finger in the air. "Wait a moment. I may be able to solve this."

Sara rose and went to the front desk to find Sean attending two couples apparently checking in. She waited, shifting from one foot to the other, hoping Sean would welcome her plan.

Once he finished, he turned to her. "What can I do for you, miss?" He winked, sending a warm quiver up her spine.

"Madison tells me you must work late."

Sean hung his head, his shoulders sagging. "Yes, now and then guests come on the evening train, and I must stay late to assist the night staff. My office is too cramped for her. No place to play. No one to play with." He sighed.

"I was wondering if I could help. I could take her home with me, and you can pick her up when you're done. What do you say?" Sara held her breath.

Sean's eyes glistened. Tears of happiness or embarrassment?

Slowly, he nodded, and his lips turned into a smile. "That is kind of you. And after a long day's work. Are you sure?"

Sara nodded furiously. "Yes. I'd love her company. And I'd be pleased to have you not worry about her."

Sean took her hand and kissed it. "Thank you ever so much. I don't know how to repay you, but I'll find a way."

"No need. Really. Just come when you can."

Sean explained his daughter's bedtime routine and warned her about Madison's propensity to wander. After receiving the advice, Sara hurried to fetch Madison and take her home to Ann's. But when she returned to the tree where she'd found the child just minutes before, Madison was gone!

CHAPTER 5

Minutes later, Sara found Madison on the dock, casually chatting with the fishermen who were bringing in their catch. Sara tried to keep the fear from her voice as she tapped Madison's shoulder. "Wee one. You gave me a fright. I didn't know where you'd gone."

Madison's confusion drew her eyebrows together and a frown to her lips. She shrugged, pointing to a boatload of fish. "They had a great haul today. Cook will be pleased. Fresh fish are always the best."

Precocious child.

Sara took her hand and squeezed it. "Since your papa has to work, he said we can spend the evening together. How would you like that?"

Like the morning sunrise, the child's face beamed. "Oh yes! Where shall we go?" She tugged Sara off the dock, onto the well-groomed lawn.

"Let's go to Ann's Café. I live just above it." Sara frowned at the rough men shouting and spitting into the water. "Do you always wander off like this?"

Madison nodded. "Papa says I must stay on the Crossmon property, but yes. I'm a big girl, and he trusts me."

"So near the river? It can be dangerous."

Madison waved a hand. "Oh, I know all about the currents and such things. And besides, the fishermen and boatmen and gardeners are all my friends. We look out for each other."

Sara laughed at the child's too-grown-up perspective and swung her arm playfully. "Still. You must be careful, wee one."

Madison sighed. "Yes, ma'am. I will." They walked a few moments in silence, but not for long. The lassie rubbed her belly. "I'm hungry."

"Me too. Miss Ann will have supper ready when we get there. She's a fabulous cook."

"When I grow up, I'm going to be a pastry chef, just like Chef LaFleur and you." Madison flashed her that toothless grin Sara loved so much.

When they reached the café, Sara peeked through the window's wispy white curtains to tables covered with checkered cloths and the café's usual patrons of bachelors and widowers.

Ann poured coffee into a man's cup, brushing a white strand of hair off her face before noticing them. "Goodness! Who do we have here?"

Madison's eyes darted around the room. "I'm Madison Graham. It's pretty here. The walls of your café match my dress." She grasped the sides of her yellow dress, curtsied, and put out her hand. "I work with Miss O'Neill and Papa at the Crossmon House."

Ann grinned at Sara and turned to the child, her eyes twinkling with amusement. "Do you, now? Well, I expect you're mighty hungry, working so hard and all."

Madison nodded, smiling. "Oh yes. It's been a rather busy day."

70

Ann laughed, patting her on the head. Then she turned to Sara, reaching for her daily hug. "And how did you fare today?"

Sara shrugged. "Fine. We made *callisons* and crème brûlée."

Ann sighed. "My husband bought me a box of *callisons* when we visited Montreal, oh, a dozen years ago. Never made them, though." A faraway look said she had retreated to the memory.

Sara tugged Madison toward a table. Settling the child in a chair, she whispered, "Wait here, and I'll bring you some lemonade."

Madison licked her lips. "Thank you, Miss Sara."

Sara passed by Ann, who held her hands to her massive chest as she gazed out the window, apparently swept up in memories of Montreal. Or her late husband. When Sara got to the kitchen, she poured two glasses of lemonade and returned to Madison, who was busy counting the yellow checks on the table.

"I counted seventy-nine, then lost count." The girl took the glass from Sara, nodded, and enjoyed a long drink. "Thank you."

Ann joined them and heaved herself down on the empty chair. "The customers are content at the moment, thank goodness. Dickie brought me some perch, so I've pan-fried the lot of them. Want some?" She turned her attention to Madison, quirking a brow.

The girl wiggled in her chair, scooting up to sit on her knees. "Yes. Please."

Sara motioned for Ann to stay where she was. "I'll get our plates. You rest a bit and visit with this wee imp." She winked at Madison and scurried to the kitchen, filled two plates, and returned to find the two laughing gaily, Ann appearing as happy as Sara had seen her in a long time. She set the plates on the table and sat down.

Ann swept a stray curl from her forehead, cutting a glance at Madison. "She's an entertaining one."

Sara giggled. "That she is. Miss Madison is the highlight of my days at Crossmon."

Madison reached out to both women, ready to pray and partake. Apparently, no time for chit-chat. Sara took her hand and bowed to offer the blessing, but Madison began. "Dear God, thank you for my friends and this food. Please help Papa to get done with work soon. Amen."

"Thank you, child." Ann glanced around the room. "If you'll excuse me, I have customers to attend."

Madison nodded as she chewed, her eyes dancing with delight.

Sara laughed. "Let me know if I can help."

Ann waved her hand. "I've managed by myself for near ten years now. You enjoy this angel."

"I will. Thanks, Ann." Sara tasted the perch first, savoring every bite. "Isn't this yummy?"

Madison dabbed her lips with a napkin, just like a well-trained lady would. "It is. Daddy's not near as good a cook as Miss Ann."

"Do you want to learn to cook like this or only bake pastries?" Sara wanted to know all about this child.

Madison looked at the ceiling for a moment and then smiled at Sara. "Both." Case closed. "Someday, I want to be a Crossmon chef and wear that funny hat and long, white apron."

"The chef's hat is called a *toque* and keeps hair from falling into the food. A short *toque* like mine shows that I am an assistant, and tall *toques* are for the top chefs like Chef LaFleur and Chef." Sara kept a straight face, trying not to reveal her dislike for her boss.

"*Toques* ... are so fancy with all their pleats." The girl took a bite of her carrots.

Sara nodded. "They have one hundred and one folds that represent the many different ways to cook eggs."

Madison blinked, setting down her fork. "Really? I only know scrambled, sunny side up and ..." Her little face scrunched up as she counted. "I guess I have a lot to learn."

Sara covered her mouth to mute her laugh. "We all do. Never stop learning, wee one." She swallowed her amusement. "The white chef's coat is worn by the head chefs to protect them from burns and stains, to show how clean the kitchen is, and to show how important the chef is. The rest of us wear an apron for protection."

"Well, then, I want a white coat too." Madison finished her mashed potatoes and set her fork at ten and four on her plate. She daintily wiped her mouth and returned the napkin to her lap, but it fell on the floor. "Dear me. That won't do."

Sara chuckled as she chewed, watching the lassie get out of her chair and pick up her napkin. But just as she was returning to sit, she looked toward the door and squealed. "Papa! You're here!"

Sara turned to see Sean walking through the door, his handsome face beaming, his arms spread wide to receive his daughter. Sean's fatherly affection reminded her of her own papa, and her heart skipped a beat.

~ ~ ~

Sean gathered Madison in his arms, hugging her tight and lifting her into his arms. Over her shoulder, he bobbed his head and tossed Sara a smile. His heart thumped at the sight of her, her gentle eyes returning his greeting. She rose as he joined her.

"Thank you for watching my girl."

Sara waved toward the table. "My pleasure. Will you join us?" Her eyes seemed to beg him to stay. He'd like nothing more.

He set Madison down and moved to an empty place. "If I'm not imposing."

Madison patted his hand. "Miss Ann said she had cobbler for us. But you have to eat all your dinner before you can have some." She pointed to her plate. "I ate all of mine."

Sara shook her head. "She's a corker. Ne'er seen the like of it."

Sean reached over to tickle Madison under the chin. "You can say that again."

His daughter giggled. "What's a *corker*?"

Sara patted her hand. "An adorable, enjoyable, funny, delightful darling, that's what."

Sean's pulse quickened, and perspiration tickled his brow. He swiped it with his napkin. *Sara's a corker too.*

Sara rose from her chair. "I'll be right back."

What was it about this woman that made him feel like a sentimental schoolboy? *Everything.*

"Sara's so nice, Papa. You should marry her, and she can be my mama."

He froze, furiously scanned the room hoping no one heard the comment, and turned a scolding eye to his daughter. "Hush, child."

Madison pursed her lips, frowning an apology.

Sara returned with a pretty smile on her face, a plate of food and a glass of lemonade in her hands. "I wasn't sure if you'd like coffee, but seeing it's so warm this evening, I thought this would be most refreshing."

Sean grinned, motioning for her to join them. "It's perfect. Your smile reminds me of an Irish saying, 'Continual cheerfulness is a sign of wisdom.'"

Sara's cheeks turned a pretty pink, and she batted her long lashes. "Why, thank you, kind sir. But I think I'm far from a state of wisdom."

"There are different degrees of wisdom, lass." He pointed to his daughter with a tilt of his fork. "This one is too wise for her own good sometimes, but you seem to have a fairly balanced measure of wisdom." He took

77

another bite. "This is delicious. We'll have to come here more often."

Nearby, a sing-song voice offered agreement. "And I hope you do."

He swallowed, turning to see a middle-aged woman in an apron. "I'm Ann, the owner of the café." She put out her hand, and he stood, shaking it.

"Sit, sit. Eat, eat." It wasn't a request. He sat.

"So this little sweetheart is yours? Good for you. Raisin' her as a little lady, I see." Ann stroked Madison's hair, and the child beamed at her.

I must make more time for Madison to be with wise women. But how?

"Papa, hurry. I want some cobbler. Please?" Madison licked her lips, strumming her fingers on the table.

He chuckled. "Last bite." Dramatically, he forked a carrot and the last piece of fish and popped it into his mouth. "Done." He set the fork on his plate and patted his lips. With three females watching him, he could barely swallow.

"Ten and four, Papa. Ten and four." Madison folded her arms over her chest, imploring him to comply.

"See what I mean?" He adjusted his fork and knife to its proper place and gave Sara and Ann an eye roll.

Both of the women burst out laughing, then quickly covered their mouths.

"I'll get our cobbler." Sara turned toward the kitchen.

Madison hopped down from her seat. "I'll help you."

Sara opened her hand to receive Sean's daughter's, and off they went.

Sean reached for his money as Ann picked up dishes, but she waved it away. "It's on me tonight. Your girl is an angel. However do you do it?"

"Thank you. The Lord gives me just enough grace for each and every day." He let out a deep sigh and rolled his shoulders.

Ann gave his back a pat, just like his mother used to do, and with it a whisper of longing niggled at him. Ann searched his face. "Mr. Graham, are you all right?"

He nodded, forcing his thoughts back to her. "Yes. Thank you."

Ann scanned the room and sat in the empty chair. "May I speak openly, please?"

"Of course, ma'am." Sean tucked his billfold back into his pocket.

"Raising a daughter is challenging, to be sure, and as she gets older, it'll only get harder. Maybe it's time to allow the good Lord to find her a mother."

"I … well … am too busy to think of such things." Sean stared at the table.

Ann glanced up and smiled as Madison and Sara came their way. "Sara's such a fine young woman, all alone in the world. And how she loves that wee one."

Sean blinked, searching for a reply. But he found none.

Ann rose and gave his shoulder another pat. "Enjoy the cobbler. All of you."

"Papa. It's peach. Your favorite." Madison dipped her spoon into the dessert, breaking through the golden crust to get to the gooey fruit. She scooped up a too-big spoonful and shoved it into her mouth. "Yum!"

"Smaller bites, darlin'. Remember your manners." He winked at his daughter, glancing at Sara to see her lick her spoon. She took another bite, closing her eyes.

"Yum! Ann's cobbler is heavenly." Sara opened her eyes and blushed, catching him staring at her.

His face burned.

"You're all red, Papa." Madison now stared at him.

"'Tis a warm, summer's eve, I expect." He looked down at his bowl and took another bite of his dessert.

As if to rescue him, Sara tugged up her shirtsleeves and fanned her face with her hands. "Yes. Maybe a stroll in the cool breeze would help?"

Sean scooped up the last bite of cobbler, swallowed, and wiped his mouth. "A fine idea. Shall we?"

Madison agreed with great enthusiasm, so they rose to thank Ann before Sean held the door for his lovely companions. As Sara ushered Madison in front of her, Sean's eyes widened. The lace of her sleeve had fallen away to reveal an angry blue bruise on her wrist.

CHAPTER 6

At the shock on Sean's face, Sara glanced down at her discolored wrist. She slid her sleeve over it, and feeling heat flame her cheeks, she stared at the floor. What would she say if he asked her about it?

Sean reached for her hand and gently pulled back her sleeve. "Where did you get this, Sara?"

She couldn't lie, but if she told the truth? "I … I didn't do something quite right." There. Not a lie.

"What happened, dearie?" Ann had joined them, concern etching her face.

Sara tried to shrug it off. "It's nothing. Stop fussing over me." She pulled her hand from Sean, covered the bruise with her shirtsleeve, and feigned nonchalance. "Let's take that walk before it gets dark."

Ann cast her a piercing gaze. She'd ask more later. Of that Sara was sure. But she sent up a silent prayer that Sean would not.

Sara gave Ann a half hug. "Be back soon. Thank you for the wonderful meal."

Ann patted her cheek in return.

Sean thanked her as well, and Madison threw her arms around the woman. "It was the best cobbler ever. Better than Chef's. Thank you, Miss Ann."

Ann waved as the three exited the café and headed toward the public dock. Madison took her place between them and grasped their hands as she'd done the night before. They walked almost the entire way in silence, even Madison being unusually quiet.

How should she navigate her growing difficulties with Chef LaFleur? If Sean or Ann confronted the man with any suspicions, she'd pay dearly. Her heart picked up its pace until she feared it might jump out of her chest. She put her free hand on it, willing it to slow.

Madison stopped in her tracks and squeezed her hand, pulling Sara from her musings. "Are you all right, Miss Sara? You look like a ghost."

Sara blinked. Twice. Then she looked down at the little girl and pasted on a smile. "I'm fine. Just pondering a thing or two." She glanced at Sean, who held the same concern in his dark eyes.

He pointed to the sandy beach ahead. "Madison, why don't you go and collect a few pretty stones before we go home?"

"Sure, Papa." The child let go of their hands and skipped a few feet ahead of them before turning back. "Wanna help me, Miss Sara?"

Sara nodded and took a step toward her, but Sean gently grabbed her arm and shook his head. "You go ahead, wee one. I want to speak with Miss Sara."

Oh no! She watched Madison skip to the sand and begin her search, wishing she could join the child.

"Sara. I think I know where that bruise came from. It's not just an innocent bump—it has a fingerprint shape." He took her hand and kissed the top of it, sending shivers through her body. Then he tenderly lifted her sleeve to expose the black-and-blue mark. "There. See." He pointed to a bruise the size of his thumb. "I've seen these. On my mother."

She couldn't look at him. Couldn't expose Chef and lose her job. How would she ever fulfill her dream? What would she do? Ann didn't need her help, and she didn't want to be a helpless, old maid for the rest of her life. She was meant to create works of art in the kitchen, and she knew it. A bit of abuse was just the cost of learning the skills she needed. Nervous energy coursed through her veins, ire rising in her thoughts.

Sean broke into them. "My father imbibed too much, too often. When he did, we all received this kind of treatment. The pain that comes from it is not just physical, Sara, and it lasts a lifetime. I cannot abide it for you." He rubbed his forefinger over the bruise before letting go of her hand. "You mustn't allow it, Sara. From anyone. The Good Book says to delight thyself also in the LORD; and He shall give thee the desires of thine heart. He can give you your dreams without being hurt by that scoundrel."

Who was he to tell her what to do?

She pulled her hands from his and shoved them in her skirt pockets, shaking her head. "Don't preach to me! If this is what it takes to become a pastry chef, then that's how it must be." She thrust her bruised arm toward him and pulled it back, her face burning. "Chef LaFleur is a brilliant man, an artist! And he is teaching me all he knows. He can provide me with a wonderful future if I'll but learn from him. Most of the time, he's just fine to work for, and I'm learning more and more every day." She gulped in a breath, her heart racing. "And who are you to scold me? You are not my father, sir, and this is none of your business. Do not meddle where you don't belong!" Glaring, she turned on her heel and broke into a run back toward the café.

~ ~ ~

Sean was only trying to help. How could he protect the woman if she wouldn't let him? Wouldn't admit she needed help? He had to find a way before something worse happened.

Madison hollered from the beach. "Where's Miss Sara going, Papa? She didn't even say goodbye."

Sean put a finger to his lips to warn her not to yell in public. Thankfully, she got the message. He joined her in the sand, bent down, and picked up a piece of quartz, handing it to her. He kept his tone casual. "She needed to go home, darlin'."

Madison tilted her head and pursed her lips. She stared at him for a moment and then clicked her tongue. "Did you make her mad?"

"Afraid so. Let's head home. It'll be dark soon."
He shrugged, brushing the sand off Madison and
surveying the stones she'd found. "You've some pretty
ones. Like you."

"Papa, don't make her mad. I like her."
Madison pouted but slipped her hand in his.

They walked the nearly six blocks in silence,
Sean lost in his concerns and Madison trudging wearily
beside him. His small clapboard home never looked so
lonely and empty as it did just then, but before long, he
had his sleepy daughter tucked safely in bed.

Sean's mind swam with thoughts of Sara. And
Chef LaFleur. Sleep would be fitful at best; that he
knew. He pumped himself a canning jar of water and
went to sit on the porch and assess the evening's
events. Why would Sara defend a man who hurt her?
Surely, she could find safer work elsewhere?

Chef LaFleur. He'd come to the hotel just
months ago and quickly became a favorite of Mr. and
Mrs. Crossmon. Famous in the Quebec circles of fine
dining. Infamous for his decadent desserts. But from
the start, the man's charming smile and flirtatious ways
had bothered Sean. He'd seen the smitten sparkle in his

daughter's eyes and forbidden her to be around the man or to go into the kitchen. LaFleur could be sweet as honey, but Sean suspected there might be a sting to go with it. When the first assistant pastry chef had abruptly left to "help her family," he'd wondered if there was more to the story.

Sean pondered and prayed for a long while, finally dragging himself to bed. He'd have to keep a sharp eye on the man. And especially on Sara.

~ ~ ~

Sara had hardly slept a wink, tossing and turning, embarrassed by her outburst, angered by Sean's words. She arrived at the kitchen early, slipped on her apron, and went to the pastry station, prepared to finish the *callisons* and whatever else they'd create this day.

Sean had no right to scold her so. If that's how he'd treat her, she didn't need his friendship. But what about Madison? She'd grown to look forward to seeing her every day, to love the wee imp.

Chef LaFleur touched her neck, pulling her from her thoughts and making her jump. "Oh! You scared me."

He put both hands on her neck and began to massage it, rubbing fear deep into Sara's bones. She stepped sideways, slipping a towel to the floor so she'd have a reason to disengage him. She bent down and scooped it up, quickly moving to the opposite side of the table.

She'd turn his attention from her. Fast! She pointed to the tray of sweets. "What's the next step in finishing the *callisions,* monsieur?"

Chef's mouth turned into an ugly smirk. At first she'd thought he was handsome? Not now.

"Do not fear me, mademoiselle. I am only here to help. To teach." He cooed as though he was speaking to a tiny babe, but he gave her a glare that spoke volumes. None she'd want to read. "You shall make the icing. I shall cut them into their traditional almond shapes, exactly two inches long. Such a task may be too precise for you." His eyes narrowed as if to judge her wanting. "They must be perfect. Sublime."

Sara took the recipe, hid behind it, and read the icing step, but Chef snatched it from her hands, waving it in the air. "The icing must be smooth and spreadable.

Do you understand? Neither too soft nor too hard. Follow the directions exactly. *Comprenez?*"

"Oui, monsieur." Her voice shook as she turned to begin. She bit the inside of her cheek and blinked back tears. With a prayer on her lips, she made the frosting, beating it to just the right consistency, and with Chef's guidance, spread the frosting flawlessly over the French candy. She stepped back to admire the creations, pleased to have made her first confectionary successfully.

"Magnifique, mademoiselle!" He reached across the table to touch her, but she stepped back casually as if to stretch her back—and to shake off her disgust.

Chef pulled a recipe from his pocket and handed it to her. "Now you shall make *macarons*, a favorite of the French and a highlight to our patrons!"

Sara grinned. She'd been waiting for this moment. She had tasted a macaron twice—first at the church's ladies' tea two years ago. It was so delightful that she'd decided she'd learn more about baking. Then, on Pullman Island, Claudia had made them for President Grant, and Sara had enjoyed another. With it, her future had been sealed as far as she'd been concerned. She had to be a pastry chef one day.

Sara wrung her hands. "Oui. I've always wanted to make them."

"Very good. First you must know that French macarons are not *congolais*—coconut cookies. They are made from almond flour and meringue, and even professionals fail at making them on a regular basis. To be successful, you must measure everything precisely. Baking is an art, but it is also a science."

Sara's nerves ticked up several notches, and her palms began to sweat. If experts couldn't make them, how could she? Her trepidation must have shown, for Chef rounded the table and sauntered to her side, brushing his lips against her ear and running his hand along her waist. "I can guide you in other things, too, ma cherie."

Her nerves sparked into a wildfire, and her breath caught in her lungs, constricting them. Perspiration prickled her temples and forehead, her stomach did flip-flops, and the room began to spin. Sara closed her eyes and whispered, "Dear Lord, help me, please."

Then everything went dark.

CHAPTER 7

Sara heard voices too garbled to understand. Her head throbbed like a drum beating in her ears. What happened? Where was she?

She opened her eyes and moaned. She was lying on the kitchen floor!

Chef LaFleur's face grimaced mere inches from hers. A whimper left her lips before she could suck it back. The man was so close to her, she didn't have room to move or sit up. She felt trapped, and something in his eyes warned her to be silent.

Suddenly, Chef pasted on a insincere smile. "Let me help you up, mademoiselle." He took both of her hands and quickly pulled her to standing, causing Sara another wave of dizziness. She grabbed hold of the table to steady herself as Chef leaned into her, whispering in her ear. "Is your corset too tight? I can fix that."

Dizzy or not, Sara stepped away from him, shaking her head slowly so as not to cause more imbalance. When she touched the back of her head, something wet and sticky alarmed her. She was bleeding.

From behind her, Cook appeared with a damp cloth and gently pressed it to her head. "You had quite a fall, miss. Let me help you." The rotund older man led her to a nearby chair and bid her to sit, still holding the cloth to her head. "It appears you fainted. Are you unwell?"

Relieved Cook was tending to her and not Chef LaFleur, Sara found her tongue. "No."

He handed her a glass of water, and she took it. "You may be dehydrated, then. In such hot weather, you must drink often."

"Thank you, sir." Sara took a sip and looked around, horrified to see the entire kitchen staff staring at her. She lifted her free hand to hold the cloth to her head. "I can manage. I'll be fine in a moment, but I appreciate your help, sir." She forced a quivering smile on her lips.

She was not fine!

Chef LaFleur sauntered up, taking the cloth from her, turning to Cook. "I'll attend to *my* employee, thank you." His nostrils flared as he dismissed the man.

Cook patted Sara on the shoulder. "Very well. You take care, miss." He turned and waddled away, sending a shiver down her spine. Her only safety, gone.

"Drink that fast, mademoiselle. We are making *pain au chocolat* and *croquen bouche* today, and both are a lengthy process. That is, unless you need to find permanent rest." His flashing eyes threatened to undo her future and crush her dreams.

"I'm fine, monsieur. May I please visit the ladies' room first?" Sara needed a moment to secure her composure.

"Oui, but be quick about it." Chef clicked his tongue and turned his back to her.

Sara hurried out the door and to the only place of refuge she could think of just then. As she sucked in a deep breath, her mind spun even as her head throbbed. She dabbed the cloth to the back of her head, relieved it was free of blood when she removed it.

What was she to do? Chef LaFleur's boldness, threats, and innuendos were getting worse by the day.

But this was her moment to fulfill her dream, to make something of herself. When would she ever get another chance to learn from a famous pastry chef? Opportunities such as this came but once in a lifetime.

She could do this. She must do this.

Sara pushed back her hair, adjusted her dress and apron, and squared her shoulders, straightening her spine. Pressing her hands to her temples to will away the headache, she whispered a prayer. "Please, Lord. You've provided this opportunity. Protect me and help me to be successful. Please?"

When she opened the kitchen door and returned to her station, Chef LaFleur's demeanor had changed yet again. He smiled, almost kindly, returning to the teacher persona she enjoyed. But by now, Sara knew that wouldn't last. If only she could endure his oversight until the end of summer and receive a reference that could take her to a new hotel. Perhaps the Frontenac or the new Thousand Islands Hotel that rivaled Crossmon?

Surely, she could survive until then.

"Time for lessons, mademoiselle." Chef LaFleur yanked her from her thoughts. "To be a famous pastry chef such as I, you must always do something unexpected. Something that will delight the eye and enlighten the palate." He paused, glancing up to the ceiling. "Today, our *pain au chocolat* shall have a sprinkle of toasted almonds atop them." He handed her the recipe card.

Sara took it and scanned the writing, but Chef interrupted her as if she couldn't read. "*Pain au chocolat* means chocolate bread. It is a *viennoiserie* sweet roll—a croissant—with a dark chocolate center. It is always laminated, and we will add a few almonds when we perform that step."

Sara swallowed hard, wondering how she'd get through the day. Her head hurt. Her heart hurt more. And fear threatened to send her to the floor again. But instead of succumbing, she pasted on a smile. "Oui, monsieur." Her voice sounded hollow, unsure, but she'd not give up.

"The dough must be cold and needs a lot of resting. I made the dough last night and let it rest twice. Now we will laminate it."

Sara had no idea what he was talking about, but she wouldn't admit that to him.

"We will laminate the dough three times, which will create eighty-one layers of buttery ecstasy."

"Eighty-one? How, sir?" Sara chewed her lip, staring at the lump of dough.

Chef grinned, handing her the recipe. "You shall mix the butter and flour together while I prepare the dough. Then I will show you."

Sara did as the recipe required while Chef stretched the dough into a large rectangle. He inspected the butter, bid her to spread it on the third center of the dough, and then sent her to chill the buttered dough in the icebox. Once that was accomplished, they folded the end thirds over, pinched the edges closed, and repeated the process two more times before letting it rest again.

Sara shook her head. "This is a rather interesting process, monsieur."

"Oui, but there is even more to do. Shave the dark chocolate while I prepare the pastry dough."

Sara did as she was told while watching Chef roll and stretch the dough and then cut it into thirty-six precise rectangles. Once done, he reached over and grabbed a generous pinch of chocolate shavings. But instead of adding them to the dough, he tried to shove them into her mouth. "Taste. You must taste to appreciate."

She complied, but his breach of decorum embittered her. He scooped another bit of chocolate for himself and smacked his lips, disgusting Sara further.

Thankfully, Chef washed his hands before proceeding to add chocolate to the dough and roll it up like a bedroll. Once the pastries were all rolled, they "proofed" them, chilled them, and brushed them with egg white, sprinkling toasted almonds on the top.

Finally, they were baked, and when Chef pulled them from the oven, he swept the tray slowly under Sara's nose. "Smell heaven, ma cherie!"

Though Sara feared he might touch her with the hot tray and burn her, he did not, and she had to admit that the buttery goodness would likely taste like a bit of heaven. But it was not heaven.

He set the tray on the table and waved a hand over it, as if he were a magician. "Now, you must give it a delicate shower of confectioners' sugar." With great drama, Chef sifted the sugar high above the pastries, producing what resembled a gentle snow shower. "No clumps or globs of sugar on these wonderful creations."

Once done, Chef scooped one up and took a bite. "Magnifique!" Then he held it out for her to taste. "Try."

Sara swallowed. After he'd already taken a bite? Surely not. His finger touching the pastries he shoved in her mouth was bad enough, but after his lips touched it? No! She shook her head. "Thank you, but I should decline. My system seems a wee bit out of sorts just now."

Chef's disapproval couldn't be denied. "Your loss, madamoiselle. And since we have wasted so much time with your system failures, we now have none left to make *croquen bouche* as I had planned. Simple *sable breton* must do, so be quick about it. I must go and plan the menu for the rest of the week." He handed her the recipe card as if it were a consolation prize. Before leaving, he whipped around and warned her with the narrowed eye of a rabid weasel. "And follow the recipe exactly."

Sara curtsied, relieved to be left alone to make the cookies. She read the recipe. *Sable breton* were nothing more than fancy butter cookies just like she'd made with her mama except that you drag a fork across the cookies in a crisscross fashion and brush the tops with a beaten egg yolk.

She didn't know why they couldn't make *croquen bouche* or why she was to blame for everything that had happened, but she decided to throw off the misplaced guilt and send it to where it belonged.

He was to blame. His flirtatiousness. His threats. His wily ways.

Chef LaFleur was to blame.

~ ~ ~

By teatime, after Chef had been absent for several wonderful, peaceful hours, Sara had everything in order. She surveyed her work. Indeed, Chef couldn't have done better. The teapots were ready to be filled and conveyed to the servers. The cookies were a perfect golden brown. The *pain au chocolat* immaculate. The silver pastry tiers artfully filled with French delights and delicate sandwiches. Surely, she'd make a fine pastry chef one day.

Just as she was glorying in her handiwork, Chef appeared from his office to inspect her efforts. He adjusted several pastries, not that they needed adjusting, and declared her work acceptable. "Fine. Fine. It is time to begin. Off with you now."

Sara curtsied, filled the teapots, and took them to the serving table. A large crowd had already gathered in the lobby. She snapped a glimpse of Sean busy at the check-in and Madison working on something at his desk in the tiny closet of an office. Neither seemed to notice her, of which she was glad.

A pianist played a lovely piece of music, and Sara wished she could stay and listen. But worked beckoned, so she returned to the kitchen to retrieve the tiers of treats. With two tiers in hand, she opened the door and stepped into the lobby, but barely inside it, she slammed into something. Hard. Or rather, it slammed into her!

Sara lost hold of the tiers, and they crashed to the floor with a thundering clang. Pastries, chocolates, nuts, and sandwiches lay strewn about, Sara aghast at the mess.

Madison? She'd bumped into the child, who sat sprawled out next to her, appearing just as shocked as she was. "Are you hurt, wee one?" Sara checked the girl, ignoring the mess she'd made. Madison was more important than food.

"I was dancing to the music and didn't see you, Miss Sara. I'm sorry." Madison scooted up onto her knees.

"I'm just glad you're all right. Don't worry. Accidents happen." Sara smoothed the girl's dress.

"It is not all right, mademoiselle! You have destroyed the entire tea." Chef LaFleur's voice was so loud and angry that the entire lobby grew quiet. Even the pianist stopped playing. And everyone stared at *her*.

Chef LaFleur addressed the room. "I am Chef LaFleur and have created the most delectable wonders for your teatime enjoyment. But my assistant here..." He pointed a bony finger at Sara. "... She has ruined it all." Madison began to cry and ran behind the counter to join her papa while Chef LaFleur snapped a menacing glare at Sara before turning back to the crowd.

"Please be advised that, while we still have some delights unharmed by this terrible error, your teatime delectables may be more scant than usual. Forgive us." With that, he bowed low, one arm over his stomach and one across his back. Then he straightened and removed his hat, bowing again. "Please forgive us, monsieurs and mademoiselles."

Sara still crouched on the floor, trying desperately to clean up the mess as discreetly as possible. Tears stung her eyes, and she bit her lip to stop it from quivering. Her hand shook as she picked up a beautiful *pain au chocolat*. Ruined.

Chef would not let her be discreet. "Clean up this disaster immediately, mademoiselle!"

Again, the people around her stopped and stared, not at him, but at her. Sara nodded, tears escaping and running down her cheeks. She swiped them away as fast as she scooped up the remaining tea service, her heart thumping her failure.

Chef LaFleur gave her one last glare before returning to the kitchen with swift steps that incriminated her. What would she meet when she walked through that door? She shivered at the thought.

CHAPTER 8

When Sara finally found the courage to return to the kitchen, Chef met her at the door, grabbed her arm, and shook her until her headache returned with a vengeance. "I'll not have you embarrass me again nor touch any of my fine creations with your clumsy hands. Not today. Non!"

One of the kitchen maids had already filled silver trays with the remaining food and then took them to the servers. It appeared that there were plenty of treats to go around, if not an overabundance.

Such a fuss over an innocent accident. Yet Sara received the most severe scolding of her life.

Thankfully, she wasn't dismissed.

Instead, Chef shunned her, relegating her to cleaning the station, scrubbing the pots, and polishing the silver for the rest of the humiliating, degrading day. Chef busied himself making the *croquen bouche* with much huffing and puffing and several icy glares sent her way.

While she cleaned the countertop, Chef mumbled to her as if he were trying to make her pay for the mishap. "*Croquen bouche* will win the hearts of our patrons back from the embarrassment of your debacle. *Croquen bouche* is a stunning, towering confection of a *croquembouche*, vanilla pastry cream and caramel-dipped *profiteroles* decorated with sugared almonds. Perhaps our guests will forget the tragedy of today with this wonder on the morrow."

"Oui, monsieur. Forgive my error." Sara curtsied, humbling herself before a man who didn't deserve it.

"Another mishap like that, and you will not be forgiven. You will be done here. *Tu comprends?*"

Sara hung her head. "Oui, monsieur." With every word, look, or action, she despised Chef LaFleur more and more. Was this constant abuse worth it? She was beginning to wonder.

The clock ticked more slowly than ever. When Sara was finally done with her day, she hurried out the back door, hoping to not have to speak with anyone.

Sean appeared, grasping her hand, imploring her with his eyes. "I'm so sorry for Madison's mistake, Sara. Forgive us."

Sara didn't have time to answer before Madison grabbed her around the waist and hugged her. "We've been waiting for you ever so long. I'm sorry, Miss Sara. I hope you didn't get in trouble. I did." She shot a repentant look at her father.

Sean snapped a smile at his daughter. "There's an Irish saying, 'Dance as if no one were watching. Sing as if no one were listening. And live every day as if it were your last.' I've always taught my little darlin' to live that way, but she needn't do it in such a busy thoroughfare." He squeezed Sara's hand. "And I'm sorry for yesterday's misunderstanding."

Sara shrugged, pulling back. "Yes, well. I need to go home and forget this day ever happened."

"May we walk you? Please?" Sean grasped his daughter's hand, and they fell into step with her, even though she hadn't invited them. Before they'd taken a dozen steps, Mr. Crossmon rounded the corner and stopped them.

Sean bowed. Sara curtsied and Madison did likewise, holding out the edges of her skirt.

Mr. Crossmon tipped his chin. "Good evening. I'd like a word, Graham."

Sara took Madison's hand and pointed to a nearby garden. "Let's go and smell the flowers, shall we?"

They left the men to speak in private, but merely ten feet away, Madison plopped down in the grass. "A ladybug landed on me. That's good luck, right, Miss O'Neill?"

Sara knelt beside Madison. With Mr. Crossmon and Sean so close, she could hear their voices. She secretly watched the exchange, glad Madison had her back to them and was thoroughly engaged with her ladybug.

"I can no longer abide you in my employ if the child remains with you. She's too rambunctious. It was fine when she napped in your office, but that's no longer the case. Mrs. Crossmon, however, implored me to allow the child to be with the burro brigade staff, but only for two weeks. By then, you must find childcare."

Sean's shoulders sagged like a crestfallen peacock. "I understand, sir. Thank you for being so accommodating."

Mr. Crossmon slapped Sean on the shoulder and shook his hand. "Sorry, old boy, but we must look out for the welfare of our guests."

Sean nodded. "I agree completely. Thank you, sir."

Madison held out her hand, shaking Sara from her eavesdropping. "Wanna hold her? I've named her Lacy because I like lace."

Sara pulled her eyes from the men and took the ladybug. "That's a fine name." But then she watched Mr. Crossmon leave, disappearing around the corner. Sean heaved a great sigh so loud Madison turned his way.

The child hopped up and ran to his side. "What's wrong, Papa?"

Sean shook his head, motioning for them to head toward the center of the village. "Shall we?"

Sara joined them, handing the ladybug back to Madison. Madison plopped it on her shoulder and grabbed Sara's hand to join the three together, yet no one spoke for several minutes.

Sara's heart ached for Sean. She might lose her job, yet she could always return to the family farm with her uncle—if she had to. But Sean? He had a daughter to support. He was the head of the household. She merely had a dream. "I'm sorry, Sean."

"You heard?"

"Yes. Your voices carried on the breeze."

Madison looked at her and then at her papa. "What did you hear?"

Sean shook his head. "None of your concern, darlin'. Just grownup stuff." He took a deep breath and stopped walking. He bent down and whispered something in Madison's ear.

"Yes! Yes! Please, Papa!" The wee lassie jumped up and down, creating little puffs of dust in her wake.

Sean turned to Sara. "Would you like to join us for the church picnic on Sunday? I noticed on the Crossmon work schedule that we both have the day off."

Madison squeezed her hand. "Please, Miss Sara. Come with us." She continued jumping until her father put a gentle hand on her shoulder.

"Stand still, darlin', and let Sara think." Sean shrugged. "Excuse her enthusiasm."

Sara bit the inside of her cheek as she thought about it. After all she'd dealt with since she came to work, her first thought was to run for the hills. And after last night's argument with Sean, she didn't want to repeat the confrontation and have one more man judge her wanting. Still, with two sets of eyes staring at her with such hope, well, she couldn't very well say no.

"All right. It'll give me a chance to try out my newfound baking skills without Chef's oversight." Sara dipped her head.

Madison hugged her tightly, nearly taking her breath away. "Thank you, Miss Sara. It'll be ever so much more fun with you. Papa can be *so* boring." She shot her father an impish, toothless grin.

Sara tweaked her nose. "Mustn't be disrespectful, wee one. Your papa loves you."

Madison turned to her father. "Sorry, Papa."

~ ~ ~

After a restless night, morning offered no new hope. Sean combed his fingers through his hair. He'd searched high and low for someone to care for Madison but found no one. At least no one safe. Old widow Beason had offered, but she slept the day away. And the Chesterfields offered, but their two older sons were rascals. He wouldn't entrust a cat he liked to them. What was he to do? Maybe he could find someone at the church picnic?

Madison skipped into his room, gave him a hug, and turned around. "Button me, please, Papa. I can't reach them all."

Sean buttoned three of the middle buttons on Madison's blue gingham dress. He tweaked the ruffles around her puffy sleeves. "You sure look pretty. And you even fixed your own hair. When did you get so grown up?"

Madison giggled. "We've gotta go. We're picking up Miss Sara. Remember?" She pulled him to standing.

Oh, he remembered all right. That's why he hadn't slept half the night. Thoughts of her smile and her soft skin and her vulnerability haunted him all night long. But Sara's tender, loving ways with Madison created equally wonderful dreams. Dreams he'd had nearly every night for the past week. Dreams of her becoming his daughter's role model. Her mother.

No! He'd seen the way she admired LaFleur. The way she jumped at his every command. The way she'd blushed when he'd yelled at her the other day. Her feelings for him were obvious. Perhaps that was why Sara had defended Chef LaFleur so when he'd asked about her bruised wrist. If that was the kind of man she wanted, so be it.

But what about his daughter? His impressionable, tender child who looked up to her? She'd be crushed.

He tugged on his trousers and donned a freshly pressed shirt. Then he tied his tie in record time.

"Brush your hair, Papa. It's all messed up!"

Sean blinked and went to the tiny mirror hanging on the wall. He chuckled. "You're right, darlin'. Looks like you pulled me out of bed." He combed it while Madison looked on, giggling with amusement. Once he finished, she handed him his jacket and tugged at him again.

"Let's go. We mustn't be late. I wonder what Miss Sara made for our picnic." They hurried to the café to fetch Sara and then headed to church.

Once church was over, Sean carried the picnic basket to a grassy spot on a small knoll. "How's this, ladies?"

Madison covered her giggles with her hand, sneaking a glance at Sara and nodding with her. Once they claimed their spot with a woolen blanket, Sara unpacked the basket. "I hope you like chicken salad. And I made chocolate éclairs for dessert." The woman's gray-blue eyes twinkled with pride.

"For us? And I don't have to wait until the guests have had their fill?" Madison clapped, licking her lips as if she'd just eaten one.

Sara reached out and tickled her tummy. "All six of them. And you can take home the ones we don't eat here." She winked at the child, sending Sean's stomach into strange spasms.

He missed his wife terribly, but with time, the ache had lessened. What would it be like to have Sara as his wife? He'd thought about Sara as Madison's mother, but as his wife? Frankly, that was a new and rather terrifying thought. He stored it in the back of his brain for further assessment later and turned to watch Madison and Sara chatting happily, munching on carrots.

"I like being a family, Papa. You, me, and Miss Sara. I wish we could be a forever family." Madison's innocent statements brought Sara to nearly choke on her carrot. She coughed several times and took a rather unladylike gulp of lemonade before returning to normal.

Sara cleared her throat. "Excuse me. Must've swallowed wrong." Her face was red as the tomato slice on her plate.

Did she agree with his daughter or disagree? Regardless, he had to save them both the embarrassment of Madison's innocent words. "I do believe that this is the best chicken salad I've ever had. What's different about it?"

Sara laughed. "I add raisins and walnuts. It varies the flavor nicely, I think."

Madison gobbled up her food and wiped her mouth. "I'm done. Can we have dessert now?"

Sean shook his head. "We aren't done yet, darlin'. Why don't you go and play with the girls for a bit?" He pointed to a group of children Madison's age.

Madison kissed him on the cheek and left him alone with Sara. Uncomfortably alone. He felt like a schoolboy, unsure of what to say. He glanced at the lovely lady beside him with a tinge of pink in her pretty cheeks. Searching for something to talk about other than work, he landed on her background.

"You liked working on Pullman last summer?"

"I liked the work but not living on a tiny island. Too much gossip and going to and from the island by boat was not my cup of tea. One summer was plenty." Sara crinkled up her nose. "But Cook was nicer."

"Nicer than whom?" Sean leaned forward, but his fixed attention faltered along with Sara's gaze.

Her face turned ghostly white, and she let out a tiny whimper. "Ah … no one."

Sean turned in time to see Chef LaFleur saunter out from behind a nearby tree, just behind and to the right of Sean. Had he been watching them the entire time?

The man brazenly stepped onto their blanket, right between Sean and Sara, his back to Sean.

Sara looked up at him. "What are you doing here, monsieur?"

He folded his arms over his chest, feet wide apart. "I need you in the kitchen. Now. Seems the wench Cook gave me to fill in for you has ten thumbs and no brain. Tea is in two hours."

Then LaFleur whipped around and faced Sean, his narrow eyes threatening. "And you, sir, have no business carousing with staff. I can have you dismissed over this." He turned back to Sara, grabbed her arm, and pulled her up so roughly that Sean jumped up.

Sean's fists balled tight. "Carousing? How dare you suggest anything improper?"

Sara waved him away. "It's all right, Mr. Graham. If Chef LaFleur needs me, I should go. Please take the basket with you, and I will retrieve it later."

Without another word, Sara was in the clutches of LaFleur, who wrapped his arm around Sara's waist, walking scandalously close to her. How could Sara succumb to such a man?

CHAPTER 9

After several dark and dreary days of rain, it seemed more like autumn than early August. The foul weather made Sara cranky, and on her way to work, she hadn't expected the skies to open up and rain so early in the day, but they did. She rushed into the Crossmon House kitchen stomping her feet and shaking off the wetness.

Sara tried to compose herself, but she had to admit that it wasn't just the weather that had sent her into an emotional darkness the past few weeks. She'd avoided Sean and Madison and regretted it. They'd always brightened her workdays—until that Sunday picnic when Chef LaFleur had threatened both her job and Sean's. Now even sweet Madison seemed but a distant memory.

"You look like a drowned rat, mademoiselle!" Chef scowled. He grabbed her arm, giving her a shake and a shove toward the pastry station.

Tired of Chef LaFleur's cruelty, duplicity, and abuse, Sara could barely endure her job anymore, even though she still savored the art of baking. The tone of her answer betrayed her irritation. "Pardon, sir, but I don't own an umbrella."

That seemed to temper him a bit. "Very well. Dry off and be about your work." Chef let go of her arm and huffed, glaring at her as she escaped to the safety of the ladies' room.

Surely, she could endure his abuse a little longer, long enough to get a letter. But could she? Sara's nerves tingled with angst. She bit her lip and grabbed a towel, dabbing her hair, her skin, her uniform, and adjusting her *toque* and apron until she finally felt presentable.

Returning to the kitchen, she found LaFleur waiting for her with a satisfied smirk planted firmly on his miserable face. "Today we will make *crepe suzette* for the afternoon tea, and though the syrup be a simple mix of butter, sugar, and Grand Marnier, when we flambé it to flavor a fresh, warm crêpe, it shall be simply magnifique!"

Sara bobbed her head, returning a tentative smile. "Oui, monsieur. Crepes are a favorite of our patrons, to be sure."

"First, you will make dark chocolate sables for those who simply must have chocolate. Proceed with this recipe, and I will return by noon. Remember to cream the butter and sugar until it lightens in color, or the cookies will be dense, as they were the last time you made them. You must not rush it. A full five minutes will suffice. They must be delicate, crumbly, and decadent. *Comprenez?*"

"Oui, Chef LaFleur. I will remember." Sara waited for him to leave before letting out a groan. She rarely met his expectations anymore. Day by day, he became more negative, demanding, controlling. Yet she had to stay to gain a proper reference from him so she could move on to another establishment.

She whispered a prayer as she creamed the butter and sugar for a full seven minutes, just to be sure. "How long must I continue, Lord?"

After making the dough, she rolled it into two logs, chilled them, sliced them, and baked the cookies. The warm, rich scent of baking chocolate made her stomach growl as she cleaned the counters and gathered the supplies for the crepes.

Once the cookies cooled, she melted some chocolate, dipped half of each sable into it, and sprinkled it with chopped, toasted pecans as the recipe suggested.

Voilà! Truly, the rich chocolate sables were a work of art. How she would love to see Madison enjoy one. Sara imagined how the wee lassie would look, her eyes closed as she savored the rich treat. And Sean? His handsome face would simply shine with pleasure.

Sara missed them much more than she'd miss this job. But Sean seemed as reticent to speak to her as she to him. When she brought the tea items to the lobby, Sean busied himself or simply ignored her. Not once had he acknowledged her presence. Not once had he made eye contact with her. Not once had Madison been there to say hello. His job was more important.

Sara's heart pinched at the breach in their friendship. Though she'd heard that old Widow Winslow was now caring for Madison, she wished the child were here to illuminate her day with that impish, toothless grin and childish joy. Unbidden tears stung the back of her eyes.

"*Fabuleux,* mademoiselle!"

Sara jumped, startled that her boss had returned.

As if sensing her vulnerability, Chef LaFleur's eyes narrowed, and he touched her shoulder, sliding his hand slowly down her arm until contacting her hand. He took hold of it and gave her a gentle tug. "Come with me. I must show you something."

Sara's heart sped up until it thumped frantically in her chest. Where was he taking her? She looked at him for answers, but Chef LaFleur's face was blank. Neither a smile, nor a scowl, nor a smirk crossed his lips.

"I must show you something … something you will never forget." The man led her outside and toward the herb garden at the far end of the property. She'd been there many times to pick mint or other herbs for their baking and sometimes to gather some for the cooks. But she'd never been afraid to go there.

Until now.

The wind whipped her skirts, and the dark, billowy clouds rumbled caution. Sara chewed her lip, willing the tension from her body. But it wouldn't leave. Instead, her apprehension grew with each step. What could be so unforgettable in a garden?

Rounding the gardener's shed, Chef smirked and pointed to a cocoon under the eave. "Is nature not splendid?" He slid his free hand up her arm until he turned her face with a powerful touch.

Sara's heart quickened, fear building with each moment. Then, in a butterfly's breath, Chef LaFleur's alter ego—the one she so feared—emerged. His eyes narrowed, his lips turned to a sneer, and he let out a groan that sounded more like a dog's growl. In a flash, he grabbed her around the neck and forced a cold, hard kiss on her lips.

She couldn't breathe. Couldn't move. She trembled with the thought she might faint again right then and there. Then what would happen?

"What is the meaning of this?" The man's voice sounded familiar, but the anger in his tone set Sara trembling all the more. Chef's body hid the man so she couldn't see who it was, but Sara prayed he would rescue her.

Chef LaFleur started to release his heartless kiss but bit her bottom lip before turning a scowl to the man. "This vixen begged me to kiss her. But this is none of your concern."

Sara shook her head furiously as she looked around Chef to her deliverer. Sean? With Madison?

"You hurt her, Chef. Her lip is bleeding." Madison let go of her father's hand and ran to Sara, wrapping her little arms around Sara's skirts. Madison gazed up at Sara, her brow furrowed with concern. "Are you okay?"

Sara blinked back tears, but they refused to comply and ran down her face. She nodded, trying to compose herself while patting the top of Madison's head.

"Don't cry. Papa will help." Madison smiled weakly, lifting her hand to wipe the tears away.

Sara glanced at Sean just as his fist met Chef's stomach. LaFleur doubled over and groaned. Sara pulled Madison into her skirts to hide her from seeing the fight. Sean grabbed Chef LaFleur by the collar and pulled him to full height. "Never! Never accost a woman like that again. Especially Miss O'Neill." He shook him and held him within inches of his face. "Understand?"

Trembling, LaFleur nodded and said something, but Sara couldn't see the scoundrel's face or make out his words. Thunder rumbled, punctuating the moment with a threatening storm. Lightning bolts flashed.

"We'd better seek shelter." Quivering as if an Arctic storm had descended on them, Sara grabbed Madison's hand and ran to the hotel as fast as she could. To escape the storm or the men, she wasn't sure. She didn't care. She just wanted to find safety for the wee one and herself.

"Are you scared? You're shaking something fierce." Madison tried to stop and get an answer but Sara simply nodded and pulled her along. She decided to avoid the kitchen and instead guided the child to the back entrance that eventually led to the lobby. Chef LaFleur shouldn't find them there, but hopefully Sean would.

Once inside, Madison grabbed Sara again, hugging her tight. "I missed you so much. I've dreamed about you and prayed for you, but Papa said we couldn't see you or he'd lose his job and you'd lose yours. Why would he lose his job, Miss Sara? I don't understand."

Still shaking, Sara bent down and kissed her on the top of her head. "I don't understand, either, and I miss you, too, wee one. More than you know." Sara gave her a hug, squeezing her and planting a kiss on her forehead this time. "Somehow, we mustn't let work separate us ever again."

Madison pushed back from the hug and questioned Sara with her eyes. "Really? Truly? Are we friends again? Oh, I'd like that ever so much."

"We've always been friends, dear one. We just haven't seen each other for a while."

"Like Mama and me. She'll always be my mama, but I don't get to see her." Madison frowned, her eyes brimming with tears.

Suddenly, the door banged open, and Chef LaFleur stormed through it. His nose and lip were bleeding. "You are dismissed, mademoiselle. Immediately and permanently!" He glared at Sara, spitting blood into his handkerchief. "Leave at once."

~ ~ ~

Sean followed LaFleur, adjusting his uniform as he hurried to find Sara and his daughter. Bursting through the door, he heaved a sigh of relief at seeing the two in the hall—and the door of the men's staff restroom swinging shut behind a set of chef whites. "There you are. Thank you for protecting my daughter from such nasty business, Miss O'Neill."

"Sara. Please." Sara's eyes locked onto his, those pools of frightened gray filling his soul with concern.

"Are you all right?" Sean took her hand in his, rubbing the top of it with his thumb.

"I'll be all right." She curtsied and smiled timidly. "Thank you for being my knight in shining armor, sir."

Madison giggled. "He doesn't have any armor, and he's not a knight. I've seen pictures in Mrs. Winslow's book."

Sean forced a smile while Sara's face turned a pretty pink.

"I ... I lost my job just now." She blinked back tears, a trembling hand fluttering to wipe her lashes as she darted an uneasy look down the hallway.

"What?" Indignation pumped blood fast through Sean's veins. "That is ridiculous. Let me speak to someone on your behalf. He should be dismissed after all he's done, not you!" A knot caught in his throat as he squeezed his fists opened and closed to calm his anger. Sara had seen enough of that.

Sara shook her head. "I think it's for the best, though I'll not receive the letter of recommendation I had hoped for. I need some time to think, to sort through this." She sighed and rubbed her bottom lip with her tongue.

Sean couldn't resist touching it, and Sara shivered. He withdrew his hand and stepped back. "You should put some ice on that."

Sara glanced at the men's room door and shook her head. "Not here. Right now, I just need to get away." She removed her *toque* and apron and handed them to Sean. "Will you please return them and tell the Crossmons I'm sorry?"

Sean groaned. "LaFleur's the one who should be sorry and lose his job. Not you."

Sara raised an eyebrow, bent down, and gave Madison a hug. "I hope I'll see you later, wee one." She straightened and smiled at Sean. "Good day. And thank you again."

He touched her arm and gave it a tiny squeeze. "May I call on you? Please?"

Sara scanned his face for what seemed like several minutes. Finally, she nodded. "Yes."

With that, she turned and scurried out the door, leaving Sean to decide what to do next.

CHAPTER 10

Sara fled to the security of Ann's Café. Upon finding the dining room empty, she ran to her friend in the kitchen and wrapped her arms around her, tears flowing freely.

"Why, child! Whatever happened to you?" Ann's eyes scanned Sara from head to foot and back up again. "Why is your lip swollen? Where is your uniform?"

She licked her lips and shrugged. "I was … dismissed."

Ann gently led her to a chair and bid her to sit. As the older woman patted her hand, Sara tearfully told her all that had occurred.

Ann's face blotched red, her eyes narrow and jaw tense. "That rogue! He'll get his just due. You just mind that. As for you, the good Lord has plans for you, my dear, plans of peace and not of evil, plans to give you hope and a wonderful future. It says so in the book of Jeremiah. It's certainly not His plan to have you abused by this man … or any man, for that matter! You just stay here and work with me, and let's see what the good Lord has planned for you."

Sara smiled, grateful for her proposal but objecting nonetheless. "But you can't afford me."

"You can practice your new baking skills on my customers for room and board. Will that suit you?"

"Oh yes. Thank you ever so much." Sara stood to begin work, but Ann shook her head, grabbing her hand and pulling her back into her seat.

"You start tomorrow. Today you rest. Take a walk. Clear your mind. Find peace with God." Ann touched Sara's cheek. "But first you must eat."

Ann brought her a plate of roasted chicken and green beans. But after only picking at her food until it was cold, Sara apologized and excused herself to take a walk. She avoided going near the Crossmon House and instead journeyed to the far end of the small town, stopping at the public docks that jutted in the direction of Pullman Island. Folding her hands over her middle, she wondered how Katelyn and Thomas were doing.

She missed her best friend and brother now more than ever. If only she could talk with them about all this.

But no! Thomas would have LaFleur strung up by his toes if he knew how the Chef had treated her.

Sara's heart clenched tight. No one must know!

LaFleur was famous and enjoyed everyone's accolades. He would turn it on her, and she'd be branded as the local vixen. Somehow, she'd have to swallow her anger, her hurt, and her abuse.

~ ~ ~

Sean shouldn't work with Madison in tow. Widow Winslow had suddenly taken ill, and the woman's daughter didn't want to be bothered with the child. Besides that, Sara was hurting, and he wanted to help. What was he to do?

Within minutes of Sean's arrival at the front desk, Mr. Crossmon stopped by on his daily rounds, and Sean told him of his childcare predicament.

His employer responded with generosity. "Take the rest of the day off. Family comes first. Peter can fill in for you." He nodded at Sean's assistant, who brimmed with pride.

Sean bobbed his head. "Thank you, sir. I shall find an answer this very day."

He wanted nothing more than to reveal what had happened to Sara and expose that rogue LaFleur, but he knew better. The chef was a celebrity in the eyes of the Crossmons, though Sean didn't know why. Why would decadent pastries matter when a woman's life was at stake? But best to hold his peace for now.

Instead, Sean excused himself and fetched Madison from his office.

"Come, darlin'. Let's find a place for you to stay." He took her hand. "I'm sure the Lord has a plan."

"I didn't like it at Mrs. Winslow's, anyway." Madison wrinkled her nose. "She smelled like liniment and old socks. Besides, she wouldn't let me play except with paper dolls, and if I made a sound, she'd fuss at me."

Sean chuckled. "I know. You've told me a hundred times. School will start soon. Can you be a big girl for a little while longer?"

"Yes, Papa." Madison frowned, kicking a pebble as she walked in silence. Then she stopped short, her eyes twinkling and her toothless grin as wide as can be. "What about Miss Sara? She needs a job."

Sean shook his head. "I can't pay her, darlin'. She needs a paying job." *If only* …

His daughter's shoulders slumped, and her smile turned into a pout. She kicked a larger stone. "Awww … and I thought I'd solved the problem." The child began to cry.

"Dry your tears, love. We'll find an answer." Sean took out his handkerchief and bent to wipe the tears from his daughter's eyes. But as he did, Madison took off running. Sean followed her with his eyes.

Sara was walking their way.

Sean's pulse sped up, and a lump filled his throat. Beads of sweat formed on his forehead, and he wiped them away. What could he say to her? That imp … trying to play the matchmaker, he supposed. But did he wish it?

By now, Madison had already hugged Sara and taken her hand, pulling her toward him. Even as he drew near, he could hear his daughter's plea. "Can you watch me, Miss Sara? I'll be good. Please? Since you don't work at the Crossmon House anymore."

133

Sara cocked her head and murmured a response.

How could he afford to pay for Madison's care? How could he afford to see Sara every day and not leave his heart in her hands?

He'd grown fond of Sara, but it was becoming more than that. The thought of another woman taking Matilda's place brought two extremes—profound joy and sadness. Could he entrust his heart to another?

"Papa, can I? Please?" The child's eyes danced between Sara and Sean. Back and forth. Back and forth. "The Lord has a plan. Remember?"

Sean nodded hello to Sara before chuckling and taking Madison's hand. "What are you talking about?"

"Sara said we can ask Miss Ann if I can be her assistant pastry chef at the café. I can't get paid, but …"

Sean scanned Sara's face, her furrowed brows. She held up her hands. "Forgive me. I should have asked you before mentioning it to her." Then she turned to Madison. "It is up to your father and Miss Ann, wee one." Sara tweaked the child's nose. "First things first."

Madison nodded, pulling on the tail of her braid. "Yes, ma'am."

Sara shrugged another apology in his direction. "I'm sorry."

Sean shook his head. "It's all right. But are you sure? You know how this one can get into mischief at the drop of a hat." He glanced at his daughter's hopeful face.

"I'd be delighted, but I do need to talk to Ann." Her eyes darted between him and his girl. "Come for supper tonight?"

"Please, Papa?" Madison wiggled like a worm.

Sean put a weighted hand on her shoulder. "Settle down and wait here. I must speak with Miss Sara alone." He took Sara's hand and stepped a dozen paces from his daughter before speaking. "You've had quite a fright. You needn't feel obligated."

"I adore the wee one, sir, and would love her company. I fear she may get bored, but at least she'd be in a safe place. I'm sure Ann will agree." Sara smiled, but it didn't spread to her eyes.

"I'm so sorry for what you endured at the hand of that man. Are you sure you're all right?"

Sara chewed on her lip. "I'm not sure I'll be able to trust men for a while, but I'll be all right."

"The famous hymn writer Isaac Watts said, 'learning to trust is one of life's most difficult tasks.' I understand. I'm not so sure I can trust my heart to another. My wife's departure nearly broke me." His words caught in his throat, but he swallowed past them. "Perhaps we can learn together?"

Sara sucked in a deep breath. Her eyes darted to Madison busily drawing circles in the dirt with a stick. "Perhaps."

~ ~ ~

As the days and weeks passed, Sara's heart began to heal a little at a time. Honing her baking skills in the tiny but peaceful kitchen seemed like a little bit of heaven after the hothouse of Chef LaFleur's tumultuous kitchen.

But it was more than that.

Ever so slowly, Sara began to trust. Trust herself to care for Madison. Trust Sean's kindness and their growing friendship. Trust God with her tomorrows. Yes, He was able to heal her heart and indeed, give her hope for her future.

By the time the school term was about to resume, Sara had taught Madison how to make *profiteroles*, the *chou à la crème* kind with whipped cream or custard or ice cream as well as savory cream puffs filled with pureed meats and cheeses, which Ann's customers loved. Sara showed her how to make other pastries and cookies too. The child seemed a natural and was rather reluctant to leave her side to return to the classroom.

Madison gave her toe a little tap on the floor, hands on her hips. "It's more fun here. Can I stay? Please?"

Sara shook her head, patting her on the back. "You can still come here after school, and we'll bake now and then. We can also fix dinner for your papa and Ann sometimes. How does that sound?"

Madison's pout seemed to fill the atmosphere with sadness. "All right. But I don't see why I need to keep going. I can read, and I know my numbers."

Sara gave the child a hug. "There's so much more to learn than that, my wee lassie. Besides, you need to be with other children."

"Children are a bother. I like grownups better." Madison rolled her eyes for emphasis, causing Sara to burst out laughing.

When school started, Sara wasn't sure who missed whom more. The kitchen lacked the child's gaiety, and though Sara enjoyed Ann's company, she found herself counting the hours until Madison tumbled through the door. And the evenings when Sean stayed for supper made those days magical.

Sara began wondering what it would be like for her, Sean, and Madison to be a family. Began wishing for it and dreaming of it. But Sean made no advances; he simply remained a good friend even though something told her it had to be more.

One September afternoon, Thomas and Katelyn sauntered through the door of Ann's Café, their outstretched arms ready to enfold Sara in their love. Her brother, Thomas, was as handsome as ever, sporting his black curls under a well-worn captain's hat. His chocolate-brown eyes danced as he reached her and enveloped her in his muscular hug.

Katelyn's hazel-brown eyes twinkled, and her array of freckles danced on her cheeks as she playfully pushed her husband aside. "My turn." She reached for a hug, but her swollen belly came between them. Still, she was too skinny for her own good.

Both women giggled as Sara gently touched the hiding place of her future nephew or niece, then slipped her hand through the crook of Katelyn's elbow. "You're glowing!"

After reuniting, Sara bid them to sit in the far corner of the café and brought them each a cup of tea and some blackberry cobbler still warm from the oven. Though Sara had sent the couple a letter shortly after she was dismissed, her brother and sister-in-law wanted to know all the details. And Sara wanted to know more about their summer too.

"When we heard from you, Katelyn was still in those early months and frequently got sick, so I didn't want to bring her across the choppy channel until the Pullmans left and closed up the cottage." Thomas shrugged, giving Katelyn's swollen belly a gentle rub. "After you said you were happily working with Ann, we were at peace. Otherwise, we'd have found a way to be by your side sooner."

"I'm home!" Madison announced her arrival in the same precocious fashion she had for weeks. But the child stopped when she noticed Sara's guests and immediately clamped a hand over her mouth. She moaned a muffled, "Sorry."

"Come here, wee one. I want you to meet someone." Sara motioned for Madison to join them and plunked the girl on her lap, kissing her cheek. "How was school?"

Madison wiggled to get comfortable. "Fine." She looked at Sara and then at the visitors. Sara gave her a gentle hug. "This is my big brother, Thomas, and my best friend, Katelyn. They've been working on Pullman Island until now but are back here for the winter."

Skepticism marred Madison's pretty features. "With you? Are they staying with you? Is she going to work with you now?" The child let out a huff as if threatened by their presence.

Sara giggled. "No … they are married and have a place of their own. You will still be my assistant, wee one."

Madison's face turned from night to day, beaming relief. "Good." She thrust out her hand in acceptance. "I'm Madison Graham. Pleased to meet you."

The three adults burst out laughing, and several customers who'd apparently been listening joined them. So did Ann, who appeared from the kitchen and hurried to greet them. "You're back, dear ones! And look at this beautiful sight." Ann gave Katelyn's belly a tender tap. "When?"

Katelyn settled back into her seat. "Christmastime. We'll be staying at the Keeler place this winter while Mr. Keeler fills in as caretaker on the island and writes his book on the history of Alex Bay. Isn't that wonderful?"

Sara's and Ann's heads bobbed in unison, and together they said, "Yes!"

Ann's customers dwindled to none, and happy banter continued for hours. Finally, Sean came through the door to fetch his daughter. Sara stood as he approached, his eyes twinkling. Her heart danced a happy waltz as it always did when he came to get Madison, but then she sucked in a nervous breath.

She'd never mentioned Sean to Katelyn or Thomas!

Sean gave Madison a tender hug. His eyes scanned the couple, and he put a finger to his temple. "Let me guess. This must be your brother, Thomas, and your best friend, Katelyn." He raised his chin and grinned.

"How did you know?" Sara's heart fluttered at his perception. She'd shared so much about them, he probably knew them as well as anyone. But why had she never found a way to mention Sean to her family?

Katelyn and Thomas looked at each other, foreheads furrowed and eyes confused. Then, as if the sun rose upon both of their faces, the two grinned and began laughing. Thomas nodded, a brow raised in amusement. "Oh … I see what's going on here." Her brother stood and put out his hand to Sean, and the two shook, patting each other on the arm with their free hands.

Sean glanced at Sara and back at Thomas. "May I please speak with you outside?"

CHAPTER 11

Sean led Thomas out to the side yard of the café. He scanned the area to make sure no one could hear the conversation. He'd waited for this moment, hoping to surprise Sara, but could he speak to Thomas—a man he'd barely met—so soon, so candidly?

On the other hand, if he didn't, he'd burst.

Sean shifted from one foot to the other. "Though you may not know me all that well, I need you to know that I have come to love your sister deeply. And I believe she loves me as well. But before I made my confession to such a tender-hearted woman, I wanted to seek your blessing to marry her."

Thomas threw back his head and laughed. "I knew it! It doesn't take a Louis Pasteur to see how happy you make Sara just by your presence. She fairly beamed when you walked through that door, and I've

143

never seen her so happy as when she was talking with you. And that wee one of yours? Sara's eyes twinkle at the sight of her. The sight of you." Thomas nodded. "I believe you'll make my sister blissfully happy. Welcome to the family, brother!"

~ ~ ~

That evening, after Ann closed the café, Sean bid Thomas and Katelyn farewell. While Sara waved them off, Sean turned to Ann. "Would you please watch Madison for a few more moments while I speak with Sara?"

"I'd be happy to, young man." The twinkle in Ann's eyes revealed she suspected what he was up to. He hoped Sara wasn't so astute.

Sean led Sara outside to what had become their favorite spot to chat, Ann's rose garden behind the café. They'd spent many hours talking about this and that while Madison played with caterpillars and ladybugs and even fireflies—when they'd let the nighttime draw them out.

Tonight the stars twinkled gaily, and a gentle breeze swirled the scent of roses and honeysuckle around them, creating a magical atmosphere and giving him the courage to speak his mind. He bid her to sit beside him on the garden bench under a trellis brimming with trumpet honeysuckle.

"I spoke to your brother." Sean pursed his lips. Why did he start with that?

Sara appeared clueless. "He's a fine man. I hope you two will become fast friends."

"Or brothers." Hoping that might enlighten her, Sean swallowed.

"What?" Sara's brows furrowed, and she stared at him blankly for what seemed an eternity. Slowly, her face relaxed, but she sucked in a breath and held it, her eyes growing wide and tears threatening to brim over. She bit her lip and said nothing. Did she object?

Sean took her hand. "I love you, my fairest Sara, and I want to spend every day of my life with you. I want to protect you and provide for you and keep you safe in my arms. Please know that I'll never force myself on you like that scoundrel Chef did. While I have breath in my body, you shall always be safe, my love."

Sara let out a tiny moan but didn't respond. Why? Was she waiting for him to propose properly?

Sean rose from the bench and knelt on one knee, Sara's hand still in his. He kissed it. "Marry me, please, and make me the happiest man alive?"

~ ~ ~

Sara blinked. She'd hoped for this moment, dreamed of it, but it was still a surprise. The most wonderful surprise of her life!

"Yes!" Sara giggled nervously, realizing she would not only become a wife but also an instant mother. "But are you sure? Can I fill the void left by your wife?"

"Not fill it, my precious." Sean kissed her hand. "God's created a brand new place in my heart for you. A place only you can fill. I love you, dearest."

Sean stood and took Sara in his arms. First, he gave her a friendly, almost brotherly hug. But then he released her, stepping back to gaze into her eyes. His tenderness, tentativeness, set butterflies flitting inside her.

"May I kiss you, my love?" Sean's voice quivered.

Sara's eyes filled with tears, and her throat pinched. She'd waited so long. "Please. Kiss me." She could barely whisper the words, but he heard them.

Sean's first kiss was as tender as the flutter of hummingbird wings. He barely touched his lips to hers, but when he did, trust, longing, and desire exploded within her, and she had to hold back from pressing her lips into his. He drew back, just a fraction of an inch, and spoke love with his eyes. Devotion. Honor. Delight. That one look held volumes and volumes of love sonnets and stories. No one else mattered at that moment.

"I love you, Sara." His lips danced on hers, barely touching them again.

"I love you, Sean." She returned his kiss with the same gentle pressure.

Sean smiled and pulled her into a tight embrace, kissing her forehead, her cheek, her nose. "Thank you, my precious Lord!"

For what seemed like an eternity, Sean simply held her, breathing deeply. Saying nothing. And she held him. The scent of roses and honeysuckle and his breath mingled into a fragrance so intoxicating that

Sara's knees wobbled. He must have sensed her falter, for he pulled back and gazed at her mouth with intensity. Ever so slowly, he kissed the top lip. Then he tenderly kissed the bottom one. "I will never hurt you. I promise."

Sara looked at him and nodded. "I know. And with God's help, I shan't hurt you either."

Sean sealed their confessions with a kiss so deep and long and lovely that Sara thought she'd sprout wings and fly. After his final kiss, he took a deep breath and smiled at her. "Shall we go and tell our daughter that she's to have a new mommy?"

~ ~ ~

Sean's heart soared on the wings of the early autumn wind as they rose to return to the cafe. She'd said yes! He'd never expected to marry again. Never wanted to. But Sara had changed everything.

Her gentle nature. Her winsome ways with Madison. Her kindness, compassion, and love of learning. Not to mention her exceptional skill in the kitchen. Sean chuckled. He'd get as fat as Farmer Zach's prize-winning hog if he wasn't careful.

"What's so funny?" Sara tugged his arm, took a step, and stopped.

"Nothing. I was just thinking how your skillful baking might have dire consequences for me."

Sara joined him in laughter. "Silly man. Let's go and tell your girl."

"No, our girl." He started walking, but reticent for the moment to end, paused again. "When shall we marry, my love? We'd better decide now, or Madison will have us married this very night!"

"What about Christmas Eve? It's my favorite time of the year, and we'd share our anniversary with Katelyn and Thomas and their baby's birthday." Sara sounded so excited that he could hardly refuse.

"That's an eternity to wait, but if that's what you want, what's three months in light of a lifetime?"

Sara reached up and kissed him. "Thank you so much. I know we'll not regret it."

Sean shrugged. "We might ... once we tell Madison."

Opening the café door, Ann met them with a finger to her lips. "She's sleeping soundly, and I'm ready for bed myself."

Sara touched Ann's forearm. "Wait, please. We have news!"

Ann put her hands on her hips and grinned at Sean. "Well? Have you finally done it?"

Sean nodded. Sara scowled. "You knew?"

Ann's eyes danced with amusement. "He never said anything, but I knew just the same."

"Knew what?" A sleepy little voice questioned from the far side of the room.

Sean squeezed Sara's hand. "Come here, darlin'. We have something to tell you."

Ann whispered. "I can't wait to see her reaction. All she ever talks about is how she wants you to be her mommy."

Sean agreed. "I know. That's all I ever hear too. She'll go mute once we marry."

"Not her." Sara chuckled. "She has more words than *Webster's Dictionary!*"

Ann chuckled. "Shall we watch the fireworks?"

And what fireworks! Once Sean gave Madison the news, the child jumped and danced and whooped with excitement. Then she ran into Sara's arms and planted a noisy kiss on her cheek. "Can I call you Mama now? I cannot wait until Christmas. That's too long!" She gave her a pleading pout and hugged her father.

Sara glanced at Sean, and he winked approval. "Yes, you may."

Madison squealed with delight, her pitch so high that Sean's ears rung. He picked her up and patted her back. "Settle down, my girl, or you'll never sleep tonight."

Madison shook her head. "I don't think I can sleep until Christmas, I'm so excited. What about you, Papa?"

Sean laughed. "I'm not so sure I'll sleep much either." He turned to Sara. "Wanna change the date?"

Sara smirked, slipping her hand into the crook of Sean's arm and giving Madison a gentle pat with the other. "Nope. We made a deal. It's my Christmas present."

"And mine!" Madison said.

"And mine!" Sean said.

"And mine!" Ann agreed.

~ ~ ~

Hindsight smacked Sara in the face. Three months *was* too long. Thankfully, Sean and she used the time well, and they endured, albeit rather impatiently.

Finally, Christmas Eve day dawned sunny and mild, the skies a bright, clear blue. It was her last day with Ann, the last day of many lasts. In just a few hours, she'd be a married woman *and* a mother with a home of her own. She couldn't wait!

Ann knocked on her bedroom door and opened it. "Ready for breakfast? I made your favorite. French toast and bacon." Already dressed in her finest maroon gown, Ann was ready for the wedding.

Sara finished buttoning her dressing gown and hugged Ann. "Thank you for everything. My time here has been a wonderful healing time, and I've loved every moment with you."

Ann waved the compliment away as they descended the stairs to the kitchen. "It's been delightful for me too."

Ann had insisted on hosting a Christmas Eve wedding luncheon and closed the café to customers. The tables were set with fine white tablecloths borrowed from the Crossmon Hotel at Mrs.

Crossmon's insistence. She'd also lent them fine white china, real silverware, and beautiful serving trays.

Sara scanned the room. "It's perfect, Ann. Never in my wildest dreams could I have asked for something so elegant. I feel like a princess."

Ann laughed, enfolding her in a hug. "My pleasure, dear girl. Let's eat."

After breakfast, Sara took one last look at the capstone of her culinary endeavors, a traditional French *Bûche de Noël* they would use for the wedding cake. "The Yule Log turned out rather well, don't you think, Ann?"

"Well, if that's not the understatement of the day, I don't know what is. It's magnificent!" Ann studied it with her. "I've seen a good many Bûche de Noëls in my day, but this one surpasses them all. You've molded the frosting to look like tree bark and made perfect sugar leaves and meringue mushrooms. And the pretty red and green frosting ribbons match your dress and Madison's and finish it wonderfully. Wait until Sean sees this work of art!"

"Thank you, again, for everything." Sara kissed the woman's wrinkled cheek and watched her beam.

"Let's get you ready, dear girl. It'll be noon before you know it." Ann rushed her up the stairs, helping her don the Christmas-green gown Katelyn had made her. Ann fixed Sara's hair high atop her head, adding several carefree locks and soft tendrils to frame her face. Then she went to her room and returned with an elaborate comb decorated with tiny red holly berries and little white flowers.

"Oh, it's beautiful, Ann! However did you make it?"

"I just took my tortoise shell comb and embellished it a bit. Let's see how it works, shall we?" Ann paused and touched Sara's cheek. "You've become like a daughter to me. I shall miss you, dear girl."

Sara gazed up to see tears in Ann's eyes. She took the older woman's hand and kissed it. "And you've been the mother I've needed." Sara stood and hugged her, but Ann bid her to sit and took on a stoic demeanor.

"We mustn't muss your beautiful gown. Turn around while I place this in your hair." She did, and after the woman finished, she handed Sara the small hand mirror.

Sara sucked in a breath. She'd never felt so beautiful in all her life!

Just then, she heard a knock on the café door. Ann motioned for Sara to remain. "I'll get it. You enjoy a moment of peace before the hubbub begins."

Sara did. She thanked God for surprising her with more than she'd ever dreamed—a future bright with promise, a good man, a lovely little girl, and most of all, hope. Footsteps ascended, and a knock sounded on her door.

"May I come in?" Thomas opened the bedroom door and peeked in. "Goodness, but you're beautiful, little sister. Sean will jump out of his skin. Ready?"

"Oh, pshaw, as your bride would say. But thank you." Sara took her brother's arm and descended the stairs.

"I left Katelyn at the church. She's feeling particularly tired today. Her time is soon."

"I hope this day doesn't stress her unreasonably." Sara gave his arm a squeeze.

"Our Katelyn wouldn't miss it! She's nearly as excited about your wedding as she is about having this baby." Thomas chuckled. "Almost, that is."

Sara held her skirts as they walked the block or so to the church, where an abundance of buggies were already waiting. "So many guests? It appears that nearly the entire village of Alexandria Bay is here. However will I endure?"

Thomas patted her arm. "You'll do fine. The crowd is a reflection of all the friends you and Sean have made in the community. Just enjoy your special day."

CHAPTER 12

"She's here, Papa! She's here!" Madison wiggled beside Sean. She jumped up and down, clapping her hands and sending the entire congregation into titters of giggles and chuckles.

"Shhh ... little darlin'. We're in church. Remember?" Sean held his daughter's hand, her Christmas-red dress reminding him of a holiday flower. What a little beauty she was!

And then he saw Sara, and he forgot to breathe. His heart drummed against his ribs until he feared it'd take wing. He swallowed hard, willing it to calm. He was as bad as his seven-year-old daughter.

Sean gazed adoringly at his bride, her hair in an attractive upswept style, her hand looped in her brother's arm, and an elegant green dress accentuating her tiny, trim figure and causing her skin to shimmer.

As she came closer, eyes a gray-green hue, lips a luscious pink. An angelic expression hovered on her face.

When they arrived at the altar, Thomas handed Sara to him. "Love her well, my friend."

Sean only nodded, his voice nowhere to be found. Somehow, he located it in time to recite his vows as Sara's dazzling smile imparted peace to his soul. It didn't matter that half the townspeople filled the pews. It didn't matter that Mr. and Mrs. Crossmon had come and sat in the very front row. It didn't even matter that his daughter stood beside him watching every move he made.

Sara ... she was all that mattered at the moment. Throughout the ceremony, Sean struggled to take his eyes off his bride, to concentrate on the liturgy. God had brought him the perfect woman. A miracle.

Indeed, he could trust the Lord with all their tomorrows. And he would trust Sara with his heart.

Pastor interrupted Sean's musings. "I pronounce you husband and wife. You may kiss your bride."

Sean glanced down at Madison. So did Sara. The child sprang up and down on her toes and clapped her hands, albeit quietly, ready to burst with joy. She giggled a whispered request. "Kiss her, Papa!"

A ripple of amusement sounded from the congregation, but Sean ignored them all. He leaned in and gave Sara a slow, tender kiss, barely touching her lips. Sara returned the expression of love.

Pastor's wide grin acknowledged Sean's accomplishment. "May I present to you Mr. and Mrs. Sean Graham."

Sara turned and took Sean's arm, handing Madison her small bouquet of flowers. The child took it, and Sara reached for Madison's free hand as she bent down to kiss her on the cheek. His heart tripped a beat. His bride always seemed to make sure his daughter felt included. Cherished.

Just as he cherished them both.

~ ~ ~

On the way to the wedding luncheon, Sara swung Madison's arm. She wanted to skip for joy but tamped down her excitement, especially in this elegant gown. Besides, she was a wife and mother now.

"You're really my mama now, aren't you?" Madison squeezed her hand.

"I am, and oh so happy to be, wee one." Sara stopped, bent down, and adjusted the bow in the girl's hair. "You look like a Christmas princess. Merry Christmas!"

"So do you! I love you, Mama." Madison beamed a smile, her eyes twinkling.

"And I love you both." Sean gave each of them a peck on the cheek.

Mr. and Mrs. Crossmon stepped into their circle of three. Mr. Crossmon cleared his throat. "Excuse us, please. But before the excitement of the luncheon ensues, I wanted to let both of you know that I released Chef LaFleur from service yesterday, even though tonight and tomorrow are such important events during this season.

Sean shook his head. "I'm sorry you've lost the talents of the man. May I ask why?"

Mrs. Crossmon clicked her tongue. "I personally saw him abusing a kitchen maid." Her face turned red, her eyes fiery. "Then the maid told me of rumors she'd heard. About you."

Mr. Crossmon harrumphed. "He said you were incompetent. I should have known better."

Mrs. Crossmon's eyes flashed as she gazed at Sara. "Why didn't you tell us that you were dismissed—*because* of him?"

Sara chewed her lip before answering. "I … I didn't think it was my place."

Mrs. Crossmon took her hand. "My dear, we'd never let staff abuse their subordinates. If I'd known, he'd have been gone, and you'd still be working with us."

Turning to his wife, Mr. Crossmon shrugged his shoulders. "But, my dear, if she were still working, she mightn't be the beaming bride she is today. The Lord has everything under control. He always does." Then he turned to the newlyweds. "Congratulations, Mr. and Mrs. Graham. You must excuse us from the luncheon. We need to tend to our hotel guests." He reached into his coat pocket and pulled out an envelope, handing it to Sean. "For your nuptials … and for the troubles you've endured, my dear." Mr. Crossmon reached out and took Sara's hand. Then he bent and kissed it. "May your joy overflow this day and every day hence."

Sara's eyes brimmed with tears. "Thank you, sir, ma'am. I am blessed indeed."

Sean slipped the envelope into his pocket and took Madison's hand. He winked at Sara and mouthed "later" as she took his arm.

When they entered Ann's Café, the guests let out whoops and hurrahs, setting Sara's cheeks to flame. Someone in the crowd said, "Kiss her again, old chap!" and Sean bent down and kissed Madison on the cheek. The guests laughed as Sean feigned innocence. "Oh, you mean her?" He pointed at Sara before kissing her, his remark sparking guffaws around the room.

When it was time for the wedding toasts, Thomas wished Sean, Sara, and Madison well and prayed a blessing over the new little family. Katelyn smiled her agreement even while appearing very uncomfortable. Sara stepped close to her and whispered, "Are you all right?"

Katelyn nodded, but a flash of pain crossed her face as she rubbed her belly.

Sean interrupted Sara's concerns as he raised a glass in thanks for Thomas' toast, gazing down at Madison. "There's an Irish Proverb, 'Bricks and mortar make a house, but the laughter of children makes a home.' Sara and I rejoice that we have both."

Sara raised her glass in agreement, taking Madison's hand and giving it a squeeze. "Hear, hear!"

The room full of family and friends cheered their agreement.

~ ~ ~

The next day, Sara kissed the baby. "Merry Christmas, my precious nephew!" She held Katelyn's newborn for Madison to see. "His name is Christopher Thomas, but they'll just call him 'Chris.'"

"Oh, like Kris Kringle? That makes sense. After all, he's a Christmas baby." Madison touched the baby's tiny hand. "I know all about babies. You must be gentle with them so they don't break. But … will he always be sleeping?" Madison wrinkled her nose. "I want to play with him."

"A newborn needs his sleep, and so does Mrs. Katelyn, but before you know it, you and your cousin will be playmates." Sara handed the baby back to Thomas, who beamed with pride. Sara smiled at him. "A son. Well done, brother!"

"I'm the one who did the work." Katelyn teased. "But we'll afford him a little credit, since it's Christmas."

Sean chuckled at the banter as he stood, reaching for Madison's hand. "Come, ladies. Let's let them have some rest. Besides, I think there might be a present or two under the tree, and a scrumptious dinner awaiting us."

Madison whooped and clapped her hands, waking the sleeping child and setting him crying. Seeing what she'd done, she let out a gasp. "Sorry, baby. Sorry, Mrs. Katelyn. I guess I still have a few things to learn about babies." Her surprise made them all laugh.

Sean nodded. "Like be quiet when they're sleeping."

Katelyn took the baby from Thomas. "It's all right. It's time for his feeding, anyway. You can learn all about babies with us before one comes to your house. How does that sound?" Her eyes twinkled as she winked at Sara.

Madison glanced up at her father. "When is a baby coming to our house? I can't wait! I want a girl, please, so we can play house."

Blushing, Sara glanced at Sean, who smiled back. "All in good time, my sweet. All in God's time."

THE END

ABOUT THE AUTHOR

Susan G Mathis is a multi-published author of stories set in the beautiful Thousand Islands, her childhood stomping ground in upstate NY. *Katelyn's Choice*, the first in The Thousand Islands Gilded Age series, is available now, and book two, *Devyn's Dilemma*, releases in April 2020. *The Fabric of Hope: An Irish Family Legacy* and her *Christmas Charity* novella are available now. Visit www.SusanGMathis.com for more.

Susan is also a published author of two premarital books with her husband, Dale, two children's picture books, a dozen stories in compilation books, and hundreds of published articles. Before Susan jumped into the fiction world, she served as the Founding Editor of **Thriving Family** magazine and the former Editor/Editorial Director of 12 Focus on the Family publications. Her first two published books were nonfiction, co-authored with her husband, Dale. *Countdown for Couples: Preparing for the Adventure of Marriage* with an Indonesian and Spanish version, and *The ReMarriage Adventure: Preparing for a Life of Love and Happiness*, have helped thousands of couples prepare for marriage.

Susan is also the author of two picture books, *Lexie's Adventure in Kenya* and *Princess Madison's Rainbow Adventure*. Moreover, she is published in various book compilations including five *Chicken Soup for the Soul* books, *Ready to Wed, Supporting Families Through Meaningful Ministry, The Christian Leadership Experience,* and *Spiritual Mentoring of Teens.* Susan has also several hundred magazine and newsletter articles.

Susan is vice president of Christian Authors Network (CAN) and a member of American Christian Fiction Writers (ACFW). For over twenty years, Susan has been a speaker at writers' conferences, teachers' conventions, writing groups, and other organizational gatherings. Susan makes her home in Colorado Springs, enjoys traveling globally with her wonderful husband, Dale, and relishes each time she gets to see or Skype with her four granddaughters.

KAY'S ECLAIRS AU CHOCOLATE

Preheat oven to 375° F and lightly grease two large baking sheets. Makes twelve éclairs.

Choux Dough

½ cup butter
1 cup water
¼ teaspoon salt
1 cup all-purpose flour
4 eggs
To make:

• In a medium saucepan, heat butter, water, and salt to boiling. Remove from heat and add flour all at once. Stir until mixture forms a ball.

• Add eggs, one at a time, beating until the batter is smooth. Cool slightly.

• Drop by one-fourth cupsful onto cookie sheet two inches apart, in rows six inches apart to make ten eclairs. Form into a rectangle and round the edges. (You can also use a pastry bag.)

• Bake for 40 minutes, until the éclairs puff up and turn golden brown. Turn off oven and let them sit in the cooling oven for 10 minutes.

• Remove from oven and cool on a wire rack for 20 minutes before filling.

• Make Pastry Cream.

Pastry Cream

¾ cup sugar
¼ cup all-purpose flour
¼ teaspoons salt
1 ½ cups whole milk
6 egg yolks
3 tablespoons cornstarch

1 ¼ teaspoon vanilla (or almond flavoring)

1 ½ cups heavy or whipping cream

To make:

• In a saucepan mix sugar, flour and salt. Add milk. Heat mixture until it thickens and boils (about ten minutes). Boil for one minute.

• In a bowl, whisk together the egg yolks. Stir yolks into mixture.

• Cook over medium-low heat, stirring constantly, until mixture thickens and coats a spoon. (Do not boil.)

• Remove from the heat, stir in vanilla, and chill for about two hours before filling pastry.

• Beat whipping cream to stiff peaks and gently fold into custard before filling eclairs.

• Make chocolate glaze.

Chocolate Glaze

2 squares of semisweet chocolate

2 tablespoons butter

1 cup confectioners' sugar

3 tablespoons milk

To make:

• In a small saucepan, melt butter and chocolate then stir in sugar and milk until smooth. Remove from the heat immediately. Stir in almond flavor and let cool for about 15 minutes, stirring occasionally.

Assembling the Éclairs

• Slice off about one-third of the top of each shell and fill with cream.

• Replace tops and spread with glaze. Refrigerate until serving.

BOOKS BY SUSAN G MATHIS

Katelyn's Choice
Book 1 of the Thousand Islands Gilded Age series
Available now!

Katelyn Kavanagh's mother dreamed her daughter would one day escape the oppressive environment of their Upstate New York farm for service in the enchanting Thousand Islands, home to Gilded Age millionaires. But when her wish comes true, Katelyn finds herself in the service of none other than the famous George Pullman, and the transition proves anything but easy.

Thomas O'Neill, brother of her best friend, is all grown up and also working on Pullman Island. Despite Thomas' efforts to help the irresistible Katelyn adjust to the intricacies of her new world, she just can't seem to tame her gossiping tongue—even when the information she's privy to could endanger her job, the 1872 re-election of Pullman guest President Ulysses S. Grant, and the love of the man of her dreams.

Book 2, *Devyn's Dilemma*, coming April 2020

1910, Thousand Islands, New York. Others may consider The Towers castle on Dark Island an enchanting summer retreat, but to Devyn McKenna, it's a prison. Yet as she works as a maid for Frederick Bourne, former president of the Singer Sewing Machine Company, her life blossoms under the kindness of his family and fascinating entrepreneurs such as J.P. Morgan, Thomas Lipton, and Captain Vanderbilt. But more than anything, the growing friendship of Mr. Bourne's valet, Brice McBride, begins to pry away the painful layers that conceal Devyn's heart.

Brice is drawn to the mysterious Devyn even though he's certain she's hiding a secret, one far more dangerous than the clues they find in The Towers that hint of a treasure on the island. When Devyn is accused of stealing Bourne's investment in Vanderbilt's New York City subway expansion, he might not be able to protect her.

Book 3, *Peyton's Promise*, coming soon

The Fabric of Hope: An Irish Family Legacy
Available now!

An 1850s Irish immigrant and a twenty-first century single mother are connected by faith, family, and a quilt. Will they both find hope for the future? After struggling to accept the changes forced upon her, Margaret Hawkins and her family take a perilous journey on an 1851 immigrant ship to the New World, bringing with her an Irish family quilt she is making. A hundred and sixty years later, her great-granddaughter, Maggie, searches for the family quilt after her ex pawns it. But on their way to creating a family legacy, will these women find peace with the past and embrace hope for the future, or will they be imprisoned by fear and faithlessness?

Christmas Charity—an Irish Brides novella, book 1
Available now!

Susan Hawkins and Patrick O'Neill find that an arranged marriage is much harder than they think, especially when they emigrate from Wolfe Island, Canada, to Cape Vincent, New York, in 1864, just a week after they marry—with Patrick's nine-year-old daughter, Lizzy, in tow. Can twenty-three-year-old Susan Hawkins learn to love her forty-nine-year-old husband and find charity for her angry stepdaughter? With Christmas coming, she hopes so.

**Sign up for her newsletter
at <u>www.SusanGMathis.com</u>**

AND PLEASE CONSIDER WRITING AN
AMAZON REVIEW.

IT'S THE VERY BEST GIFT YOU CAN GIVE AN
AUTHOR.

THANKS!

27845993R00102